CREATURES OF CLAY

PATRICK MOODY

This is a work of fiction. Names, characters, places, and incidents either are the product of the author's imagination or are used fictitiously. Any resemblance to actual persons, living or dead, events, or locales is entirely coincidental.

Copyright © 2021 by Patrick Moody

All rights reserved. No part of this book may be reproduced or used in any manner without written permission of the copyright owner except for the use of quotations in a book review. For more information, address: patmoody2@gmail.com

First paperback edition June 2021

Anuci Press edition March 2024
www.anuci-press.com

Cover design by Adrian Medina

ISBN 979-8-9896198-3-2 (paperback)
ISBN 979-8-9896198-7-0 (ebook)

Praise for Patrick Moody

"Patrick Moody paints compelling human portraits with his prose that morph into the stuff of nightmares."
  -John Ballentine, Creator of *Campfire Radio Theater*

"A love letter to classic horror tales, teeming with action and 80's nostalgia. This book will make you want to grab the flashlight and go hunt some monsters."
  -Kim Ventrella, author of *The Secret Life of Sam*

"For fans of Bradbury, Carpenter, and all things Stephen King, Patrick Moody's *CREATURES OF CLAY* is a nostalgic dream, a throwback coming-of-age story of small-town horror in which a ragtag group of children reckon with a malevolent force that changes their lives forever. Familiar enough to be comforting, yet different enough to inspire admiration, I found myself rooting for The Crypt Crew. You will too."
  -Kealan Patrick Burke, Bram Stoker Award-winning author of *KIN* and *SOUR CANDY*

"With Creatures of Clay, Patrick Moody weaves an exciting and scary tale for monster kids of all ages. If this book doesn't make you want to start a Crypt Crew of your own... you might be a golem!"
  -Matt Weinhold, writer: *Beware the Batman* (Cartoon Network), *Stan Against Evil* (IFC), co-host of *Monster Party Podcast*

"Moody packs his cemetery with magic and monsters and makes digging up the dead a lot of fun."
  -J.W. Ocker, Edgar Award-winning author of *Death and Douglas*

"Deliciously eerie and heartfelt, *The Gravedigger's Son* sweeps you into a world of Diggers, Voicecatchers, and Weavers, where only a reluctant young gravedigger can save the day."
  -Sarah McGuire, author of *Valiant*

For Meg

The Glow Worm (Das Glühwürmchen)

Verse 1: When the night falls silently
The night falls silently on forests dreaming,
Lovers wander forth to see,
They wander forth to see the bright stars gleaming.
And lest they should lose their way,
Lest they should lose their way, the glow-worms nightly
Light their tiny lanterns gay,
Their tiny lanterns gay and twinkle brightly.
Here and there and everywhere, from mossy dell and hollow,
Floating, gliding through the air, they call on us to follow.

Chorus: Shine, little glow-worm, glimmer,
Shine little glow-worm, glimmer!
Lead us, lest too far we wander,
Love's sweet voice is calling yonder!
Shine, little glow-worm, glimmer,
Shine, little glow-worm, glimmer
Light the path below, above,
And lead us on to love.

Verse 2: "Little glow-worm, tell me pray,
Oh glow-worm, tell me pray, how did you kindle,
Lamps that by the break of day,
That by the break of day, must fade and dwindle?"
"Ah, this secret, by your leave,

This secret, by your leave, is worth the learning!
When true lovers come at eve,
True lovers come at eve, their hearts are burning!
Glowing cheeks and lips betray, how sweet the kisses tasted!
Till we steal the fire away, for fear lest it be wasted!"
English Lyrics by Lilla Cayley Robinson / Music by Paul Lincke

A Fourth of July to Remember

Stark Falls, New Hampshire
July 4, 1985

Quinn Katz awoke to the sound of screams.

He jerked upright, swinging his feet off the mattress and nearly stepping in last night's bowl of cereal as the sound faded down the hall.

Morning sunlight spilled into the room, making it easier to navigate around clothes, comics, and paperbacks strewn about the floor in haphazard piles.

He stopped at the door at the end of the hall and knocked.

"Come in," the voice said. As usual, it sounded very, very tired.

Quinn found his older brother Henry sitting on the edge of the bed. He was breathing deep, ragged breaths, as beads of sweat dotted his brow.

When Quinn put his arm on Henry's shoulder, the older boy flinched.

"It's okay," Quinn said. "It's over."

Henry nodded, his eyes fixed on the floor.

"Can't get rid of them," he said softly. "I thought maybe they'd go away. I thought…" he took a deep breath, sighing. "I don't know what I thought. Sorry I woke you, pal."

Quinn saw the raised white scar that ran from Henry's elbow to his wrist, a constant reminder of that fateful day on Stark River. Quinn wished there was more he could do to comfort him. He wished there was something he could say, some magic phrase that would make Henry's nightmares stop.

Henry's dreams started soon after the accident. Quinn had asked him about it, or tried to. So many times, he tried. But Henry said he wasn't ready to talk about it.

Not yet, he'd say. Quinn said he understood, but they both knew he didn't. The scars Henry bore in his mind were worse than those that marred his skin. It would be a long time before they healed over.

Quinn liked having Henry back. He needed him.

He expected Henry needed *him*, too. When their father passed away, the brothers decided they'd always look after each other. More often than not it was Quinn who did the looking after, but he didn't mind.

Since Henry was twenty-one, he was an adult, though Quinn still had trouble seeing him that way. They were nine years apart, but he would always see Henry as that fun-loving teenager who taught little Quinn how to make the best slingshot and homemade bow-and-arrows, playing cowboys or ninjas out in the back yard or up at the Falls.

That Henry's still there, Quinn told himself. *I just have to give him time.*

The old Henry *was* coming back, slowly but surely. After all, the dreams *were* getting better.

"What time is it?" Henry asked.

"Just about eight."

"I'd better get to the station, then. Sheriff's leaving today." He let out a yawn.

Quinn nodded. "I'll make some coffee."

"You take good care of me, pal, you know that?" He tussled Quinn's hair. "I should be taking care of *you*."

"That's alright," Quinn said. He walked to the dresser and handed Henry his Stark County Sheriff's Deputy badge. "We take care of each other."

Henry took the badge, smiling.

Quinn liked when Henry smiled. *Really* smiled instead of looking happy for Quinn's sake. It didn't happen near enough.

"Right," he said. "Watch out, evildoers, here come the Katz brothers!"

Quinn laughed.

"You want a ride to Malman's?"

"That's okay," Quinn said. "I think I'll ride my bike. Stop by Hector's."

Henry shrugged. "Ah, right. The Crypt Crew, together for the whole summer. Got any dastardly deeds planned?"

The "Crypt Crew" was Henry's name for Quinn and his two best friends, Hector Delgado and Wendy Francis, since the three of them had been writing and illustrating horror stories since the third grade. Hector's sister, Maria, and her own little gang had come up with the name for them, meaning it as an insult, of course, but Quinn liked the name, and they'd used it ever since.

"A few," Quinn said. "But that's our secret."

"Hey watch it. I can bring you in for questioning, hot shot."

Quinn hurried to get the coffee ready.

He dialed in the kitchen radio to WKLT, and the voice of Rick "Madman" Wade came through the speakers.

"Good morning, Stark Falls!" he said in his crooning voice, "Looks like today will be a hot one, nice and sunny for this afternoon's parade. Word on the street says this Fourth of July is gonna be the biggest shindig this little town's ever seen. So, rise and shine, Fallers, wipe away those sleepy seeds and say goodbye to old Mr. Sandman."

Madonna's "Borderline" played. Quinn tapped his feet and went about fixing breakfast.

A few minutes later, they were at the kitchen table, dressed and ready, each sipping the hot coffee from their favorite mugs. Henry looked much better, now that he was in his uniform. One look and you'd never know he barely made it one night a week without night terrors. His thumbs were looped through his belt. The holster on his hip was empty, as usual. Henry refused to carry a gun.

Quinn wished their dad could have seen him. He was so proud when Henry and his friends had saved those kids on the river. He could only imagine how proud he'd be to see him with that shiny badge on his chest.

Quinn decided he'd be proud of both of them.

"Excited?" Quinn asked.

Henry adjusted the wide brimmed hat, then fiddled with the sunglasses hanging from the collar of his shirt. "Nervous, more like. Old man Toohey's been talking about this fishing trip of his for months." He chuckled. "Never thought he'd actually go. Can you imagine that grump enjoying a *vacation*? I don't think he knows the meaning of the word."

Quinn laughed, imagining Sheriff Toohey with a smattering of sunblock on his bulbous nose, trying to wrangle a swordfish and cursing up a storm.

He'd been the Stark County sheriff for thirty years. Quinn wondered if he'd ever retire, or even wanted to. Everyone in Stark Falls loved him, even if he was about as friendly as a bulldog with a thorn stuck in its butt. But he was getting old, and when the town council finally convinced him to take on a deputy, Henry jumped at the chance. His local fame helped. People wanted a hero for the job.

And now, Sheriff Toohey was taking his first vacation in...well, probably *ever*. Which meant Henry would be acting sheriff for an entire month. Maybe more.

"It's a tall order," Henry mused between sips of coffee. "Let's hope the town doesn't spiral out of control, huh? Last thing I need is for this place to turn into crime central. Especially on the Fourth of July. Especially today." Those last words came out forced, and Quinn saw Henry's jaw tighten for a moment.

"This place?" Quinn shook his head, smiling. "As long as the gardening and knitting club ladies don't go at each other with their hedge trimmers and needles, I think you're set, Deputy."

"That's good. They *have* been pretty jealous of each other's floats. I'll make a note of that." He mimed writing in a notebook. "Make sure Mrs. Gibbs doesn't try to poison Evie Wilson's rose beds. Send out the alert! Calling all cars!"

Quinn laughed. The only real issue facing Stark Falls, and one that Henry would have to deal with, was the old wood-covered bridge, nicknamed 'Old Rickety', which had just collapsed earlier in the week. Since it was one of the only two bridges leading into and out of the Falls, its disrepair was the talk of the town. The other bridge, that one steel and stone, was also faltering. If anything happened, there'd be no getting in or out of the town. At least not on four wheels.

Henry finished his coffee and made for the back door. "Well, wish me luck, Q. If you need me, you know where to find me."

"Yessir," Quinn said. "Down at the jailhouse with half the town in cuffs."

Henry gave him a thumbs-up. "You know it, pal-o-mine. See you at the parade tonight?"

"I'll be there."

Henry opened the door, putting on his best John Wayne voice. "Watch out, pilgrims. There's a new sheriff in town!"

Quinn sat at the table for a moment longer, listening as the car started up and rumbled up the gravel drive.

Once he was gone, Quinn raced to the mailbox. As he hoped, there was a letter waiting for him. He opened it right there, tearing the paper from the envelope. His eyes grew wide when he saw the words at the top.

From the Editors of *Tales of Terror* Magazine
Dear Mr. Katz, Mr. Delgado, & Ms. Francis

Thank you so much for your recent submission, ***"ATTACK OF THE LIZARD MEN".*** *While we found the story to be very well written, particularly the mad scientist and his henchmen, we feel that this is not the right piece for us at this time. We encourage you to keep writing and look forward to more submissions in the future.*

P.S. The illustrations by Ms. Francis captured the mood of the story very well.

Best,
Tales of Terror

"Darn," Quinn said, folding the paper and sticking it in his back pocket. They'd been so close that time. The rejection hurt. They always did. That was number... "Fifty-one," he said aloud. Fifty-one stories he'd written with Hector and Wendy. Fifty-one letters that he kept pinned on a special board in his room, all "thank you" and "better luck next time".

But, he thought with some excitement, this was the first time they ever said something good about the story. He guessed that meant something.

We're getting better, he thought. And one day, he'd see their names in the pages of *Tales of Terror*. Of that Quinn was sure, no matter how many rejections they got.

We found the story to be very well written...

Those words filled him with pride. He could almost taste them. Butterflies fluttered in his stomach as he got his bike from the side of the house and hopped on, his legs pumping the pedals as fast as they could carry him up the driveway and down the street to Hector's.

He rang the doorbell, bursting to tell Hector about the letter. Inside, he could hear feet clamoring down stairs. The door flew open as Quinn made to ring the bell once more, and he stumbled back off the front step.

Maria Delgado blocked the doorway, her arms folded.

"Hey, Maria," Quinn said, trying to peer over her head and into the house. "Hector home?"

"It's seven o'clock in the morning, Count Dracula," Maria sneered. "Where else would he be?"

"Quinn? Is that you, hon?"

To Quinn's relief, Dr. Delgado appeared in the entryway.

"Get a move on, Maria," she said, nudging her out of the doorway. "That homework won't finish itself. Get that bookbag out of the car, chica."

Maria groaned, spinning on her heels and muttering something in Spanish.

"Watch that tone!" Dr. Delgado said. "You wouldn't be doing homework on a holiday if it wasn't for that attitude of yours. And get your brother!"

"Hey, weirdo!" Maria shouted at the foot of the stairs, "your bud's here to take you both back to your home planet!"

"Don't mind her," Dr. Delgado said. "*Someone* is just upset they have to spend the next month in summer school."

Hector had been on edge ever since Maria got the letter from school. For twins, they sure didn't get along, and Maria had a nasty habit of taking out her anger on Hector. And she was angry a *lot*. Even though she was smaller, she always got the better of him in a scuffle.

Hector stomped down the stairs, passing Maria, who gave him a shove off the bottom step.

"Hey!" he shouted.

If Dr. Delgado noticed, she didn't show it.

"You excited for the parade tonight, hon?"

"Very," Quinn said.

"Just promise me you kids will be careful. I'll be at the clinic 'til midnight. Hope no one gets any bright ideas with those fireworks, like last year."

Quinn stifled a laugh. He'd only heard it second hand, but there had been quite a big deal involving high school kids, cherry bombs, and the library restroom. Apparently, the custodian, Mr. Todd, didn't think to lock up that night. While the festivities were in full swing on the town green, four toilets blew sky high, sending the librarians into a tizzy.

"Those things should be illegal, if you ask me," Dr. Delgado said.

Hector joined Quinn on the front step, his curly hair wet with fresh moose. "We'll be safe, mom. You worry too much."

Maria shoved past them, stomping over to the car and yanking the door open so hard Quinn was surprised it didn't break off. She reached in and grabbed the book bag, scowling so intently that Quinn thought it would've looked perfect next to the word in the dictionary.

"I worry *just* enough, thank you. You boys be good and give my best to Mr. Malman."

"We will!" Both boys said together and ran to their bikes.

"And NO CHERRY BOMBS!"

"You got it, Ma!" Hector yelled over his shoulder, shooting Quinn a conspiratorial grin as he threw himself onto his Schwinn. He took one sheepish glance at his sister, who was standing in her bedroom window mashing a fist into her palm.

The boys pedaled fast.

"Maria seems more sour than normal, today."

Hector let out a humorless laugh. "You think? Mom couldn't get her out of bed this morning. She made *me* go in there!"

As they rode through the winding, tree-lined streets, Quinn noticed the mean looking bruise just beginning to darken like an eggplant on Hector's arm.

Not again.

"Hey, do you think maybe you should tell your mom about that?" He nodded to the bruise.

Hector's cheeks went red, and as he rode, he tried to stretch his sleeve down.

"Won't do any good," he said. "Anyway, it really wasn't that bad. Maria has just been a nightmare since school got out. She's bummed she has to spend July writing essays with Mr. Colburn, instead of the Nature Scouts."

"Well at least you get a break from her," Quinn said hopefully.

"Maria-free from seven to three!" Hector snorted a laugh.

Hector's laughter set Quinn's mind at ease, but every now and then he'd find himself staring at the bruise. Quinn figured you couldn't find a more opposite pair if you tried. Hector was short and tubby, with a love of writing and video games, where, like most kids in Stark County, Maria was all about the Nature Scouts. She'd wear her Scout cap to school, and sometimes her sash, boasting badge after badge. Hector's parents even let her camp out in the backyard when the weather was nice. She lived for the outdoors, as opposed to Hector, who'd much rather stay inside with his comic books and a big bottle of Pepsi. Any arguments they had usually ended with Hector looking like he'd just been flattened by a steamroller.

It hadn't always been that way. One night during a sleepover, Hector had opened up, whispering over the late-night horror flick about he and Maria. Apparently, the tables had begun to turn the minute Dr. Delgado had decided to move them to Stark Falls. "Maria wasn't having it," he'd said, "Yonkers was home, you know? She had tons of friends. Queen of the neighborhood. Now?" He'd huffed. "She's the queen of pounding on me. Have to be the queen of something, I guess."

They hadn't spoken of it much, since. Hector's plain embarrassment was enough.

"Want to stay over at my place?" Quinn asked. "You know...just in case Maria doesn't take her first day at school well..."

"No," Hector said, a bit too quickly, stiffening. "Honest, Q. I'm fine. I can deal." He paused, "Any word from the magazine?"

Quinn knew his best friend well enough to know when he wanted to change the subject. It was one of Hector's special talents, although Quinn guessed you had to be good at changing the subject when your twin treated you like a punching bag. He reached into his pocket and passed Hector the note, watching him flatten it on the handlebars and read mid-pedal.

"Bogus!" he cried, a little out of breath. "I really thought we had something, there."

"Me too," Quinn said. "But hey, they actually said some nice things!"

"About your scientist, sure. But what about my lizard men? No mention of them. Thought I made 'em plenty scary, with the acid spit and all."

"You did," Quinn assured him. "They said the whole thing was well written."

"And they liked Wendy's drawings, too. That's good."

They rode down Barker Street and took in the sight of Stark Falls. The town was surrounded by the White Mountains with most of the houses set in a small valley that looked like the bottom of a cereal bowl. The looming mountains ringed the town on three sides, while the wide, frothing Stark River cut through the other. Stark Falls was small, but it was the biggest town in Stark County. The summer brought out a shock of color as pine trees covered the mountains and made them look like gigantic waves in a vast ocean of green, and dandelions dotted the rolling hills and lawns like a smattering of fallen stars.

Fulton Street led straight down the valley onto Main Street. Quinn and Hector glided down, riding past the town green. Already, people were setting up for the parade. Quinn saw the high school marching band practicing on the grass while members of the Historical Society were putting a red, white, and blue jacket on the statue of Nathaniel Stark, the town's founder. Streamers and balloons covered the bandstand, where the town handyman Mr. Arpin and his jazz quartet would play.

"Maybe we should send it to some other places," Hector said. "Like *Weird Fantasy* or *Horror Haunts*."

"I sent it to both," Quinn said. "No response."

Hector frowned at that, then shrugged.

All the letters were sent to Quinn's address for a few reasons. First, Henry didn't mind Quinn's obsession with everything horror and science fiction. In fact, he'd always encouraged Quinn to pursue it. After all, some of the best times they ever had were going to the local drive in to see movies like *Friday the 13th, Halloween, Poltergeist,* and *Nightmare on Elm Street.* Henry preferred Westerns, but he always drove Quinn when something scary was playing.

Second, Dr. Delgado would be mortified if she knew Hector read that kind of stuff. One time she found a copy of *Fangoria* under his pillow and grounded him for a whole week.

Wendy's dad wouldn't mind, she told them. He was so busy as Nature Scout Master that he didn't seem to mind anything, when he bothered to pay her any attention. Just to play it safe, she agreed that all their stories would be addressed to the Katz residence.

"I think I have our next story," Hector said. "Something my abuela used to tell us. Scared our socks off. Well, Maria's more than mine"

"Sure, tough guy."

Quinn's own grandma, who made him call her *Bubbe* and spoke mostly Yiddish, told some doozies, but Abuela Delgado's were always the scariest. Hector must have had the weirdest bedtime stories out of any kid in New Hampshire.

They pulled up to Malman & Son's General Store. Mr. Malman was teetering on top of a ladder, trying to fix the neon "SON'S" sign, which was blinking on and off.

For a moment, Quinn didn't move, just looked up at the older man as he tried to get the light working. A sense of sadness welled up inside him, even as Hector parked his bike and gave Mr. Malman a big, bellowing hello.

There was something almost haunting about it, Quinn thought. That sign that kept blinking "SON'S". Because Mr. Malman didn't have one. Not anymore. Ethan had spent the last Fourth of July on a hiking and boating trip with Henry and a few other friends.

He was the only one who didn't come back.

Exactly one year to the day. The Fourth wasn't a day of celebration for everyone in Stark Falls. Especially for the ones who remembered.

As Quinn watched Mr. Malman banging on the sign with a pole, he felt like the old man was trying to keep the memory alive. Like if that light went out, Ethan would be gone forever. With a sigh of relief, he watched as Malman gave it one last wallop with the pole, and the light beamed steady.

"Well," Mr. Malman huffed, climbing shakily down the ladder. "Let's hope that did the trick, eh boys?"

"Looks good, Mr. Malman," Quinn said.

He nodded, his eyes magnified by coke bottle glasses. He hitched up his pair of workman's overalls and ran a hand against the back of his neck. "Sure is hot. Say, Quinn, you up for fixing up some sodas?"

"Quinn's on soda duty *again*?" Hector whined.

"I seem to remember a certain young man saying he needed a break from the counter," Mr. Malman said, grinning.

"Well, that's only because it was real busy yesterday, Mr. Malman, and the soda stream broke and my shoes got covered in the syrup and, ah man, I—"

"Yes, and I had to clean the Donkey Kong machine because of the sticky buttons," Malman said, smiling, "I have plenty of work for the both of you. And if you thought yesterday was busy, Mr. Delgado, I'll have you know that Malman & Sons does some of its biggest business on the Fourth!" He clapped them each on the shoulder and walked them inside.

As Quinn stepped over the sewer grate, his sneaker caught on something sticky. He raised his foot, examining the thick strand of gray goop.

"Awful stuff," Mr. Malman said, taking him by the arm. "Been showing up a lot, lately. Come on, I'll get you some paper towels."

Wendy was already busy setting up display cases in the windows with spinners, sparklers, and poppers. Above the display was a mural on a large, stretched canvas. Wendy had painted it black, adding stars and exploding fireworks in dazzling neon pops of color.

"Looks good!" he said, taking in the display.

"Been here since six," Wendy said, hopping down off the step ladder, her *Ramones* shirt splattered with paint. "I figured I might as well do something useful. Dad got up early to get the campground all set for the Scouts." Her eyes fell to her shoes, "*And* he had a nasty phone call with Mom, so I decided to split before the real yelling started."

"What happened this time?"

Wendy shrugged. "She wants me to spend the second half of the summer with her in New York. Another gallery opening."

"Least you're not in summer school with Maria," Hector said.

"Do you want to go?" Quinn asked.

Wendy shrugged. "New York's nice and all, but lonely for such a big place. But Mom's having some of her work shown at a gallery and she really wants me there. Said it's a good opportunity for me to learn. Maybe meet some people and show them some of my pieces." She shrugged, as if she wasn't really sure she believed in what she'd just said.

Wendy always said she got her artistic side from her mom, who was a great painter. Quinn and Hector had never met her. She never came to visit, and rarely called Wendy. Quinn got the distinct feeling that she was more concerned with her art than her daughter. Wendy's Dad reluctantly supported her own artwork, but the Crypt Crew all knew he'd rather have a little Maria Delgado, eager to venture outdoors, rather than an arty kid who loved drawing monsters.

Wendy shook her head, as if banishing the entire idea. "But who knows? Maybe I'll visit over Christmas or something. What's up with you guys?"

"Got some news!" Hector said.

Quinn handed her the letter. She read it, brows furrowing, then huffed.

"Seriously? I thought that was my best stuff yet!"

"That makes two of us," Quinn said.

"Three!" Hector called.

"Hector says he has a new idea. Maybe we can work on it later?"

"Sure," Wendy said. She eyed a sheet of receipt paper on the counter. "Maybe Mr. Malman will lend me some more stuff. I used up my supplies on the last one. Those Lizard Men took up my good paints."

"You know he will," Quinn said. And they both knew it was true.

The Crypt Crew had been helping out around Malman & Sons since school got out. Not for money, but because Mr. Malman was pretty sad, they figured, and about as lonely as a person could get. Mr. Malman told them over and over that they were like his own children, and he showed his gratitude by paying not in coins, but in goods from the store.

For Quinn, it was model kits and paperbacks. Ray Bradbury was his favorite, but he also liked Richard Matheson, Stephen King, and Agatha Christie murder mysteries. For Hector, it was the arcade games: *Dungeons & Dragons*, *Ghosts 'n Goblins, Donkey Kong*, and all the soda he could drink. And for Wendy, it was paint and paper, scissors and glue, and whatever else she needed for her artwork, and a healthy stack of monster magazines. She loved the posters for the latest movies, and hoped to illustrate them herself, one day.

It was a nice arrangement for the Crypt Crew, who, as the other children in Stark Falls would say, were *indoor kids*.

"By the way," Wendy said, "did Mr. Malman show you his latest delivery?"

Quinn and Hector followed her to a wooden stand, upon which several extremely ugly and undeniably creepy dolls sat arranged in neat rows.

Hector inched forward, prodding one in its misshapen, wrinkled face.

"What are these? Shrunken heads?"

"Dried apple dolls," Wendy said. "From Mrs. Ruane. The Historical Society is trying to sell them as a fundraiser for the bridge. Mr. Malman tried to tell her no one would be interested."

"I'm sure that went over well," Quinn said.

Mrs. Ruane was the chairwoman of both the Historical Society and the Garden Club and ruled both with the iron first of a tyrant. She was mean and loud, forever shouting on account of losing most of her hearing, which she made up for by walking around with a ridiculously huge ear trumpet, a wood and gold-plated monstrosity that poked out of her ear like the shell of some giant snail. Mr. Malman called it her "demon horn", but only to the Crypt Crew, and very quietly. Even *he* was a bit scared of her.

Quinn peered at the dried apple dolls, looking at their creepy black-button eyes and their sour, puckering faces, all wrinkled and frowning.

"They even look like her," Hector observed.

"Don't let her hear you say that!" Mr. Malman called from the register. "She's making me keep those dreaded things. I'm thinking of just giving her the money and tossing them in the compost pile. If worse comes to worse, I'll get my toolbox and fix Old Rickety myself. A one-man bridge-repair!"

Quinn picked up one of the dolls, turning it in his hands. "You know, these would be good for a story."

"Yeah," Wendy said. "*The Dolls Who Wake at Midnight!*"

"Now *that* would give me nightmares," Hector said, stepping away from the display and inching towards the *Donkey Kong* machine, quarters jingling in his pockets.

"Alright, you three. It's too early for horror stories. Sodas, Quinn! And arcade games later, Hector."

Quinn stepped behind the counter and made sure the freezer and mixers were clean, then made four ice cream sodas.

While he filled the glasses, he looked across the store to the magazine and book racks. In the very center were the latest issues of *Famous Monsters of Filmland*, *Fangoria*, *Amazing Science Fiction*, and *Tales of Terror*. He grew lost in thought, staring at all those covers with skeletons, werewolves, robots, and zombie pirates, head swirling until the bell over the door rang and the first wave of customers entered.

"Oh, wow!"

Hector was dragging wooden crates from the stockroom.

"Here," Mr. Malman said, handing him a crowbar. "You'll need this."

Hector pried open the lid and dug around the packing paper, pulling out a box that he held triumphantly to the light.

"Quinn! Wendy! Look at this!"

On the side of the box, Quinn saw in big red letters: CHERRY BOMBS.

Oh, no. Hector's mom would have their hides if she knew they were anywhere near those. And Quinn also knew that if Hector blew off a thumb or pinkie, she'd have their heads along with their hides.

Hector would never admit it, but Quinn also knew that the sight of blood made him pale as a ghost.

"Got those on special order from the factory in Connecticut," Mr. Malman said. "And there's more where that came from."

As Quinn put the finishing touches on their ice cream sodas (who else would let them have ice cream for breakfast other than old Mr. Malman?) and Wendy finished the window displays, Hector was busy prying the lids off boxes marked **M-80s**, **SUPERNOVAS**, **ATOM BLASTS**, and a crate the size of a coffin marked **UNCLE SAM'S THUNDERBOLTS**, laughing like a maniac while Mr. Malman manned the counter, looking on with a smile from ear to ear.

Quinn decided then and there that this would be a Fourth of July to remember.

THE RABBI

A shadow fell over the soda counter. A loud, throat-clearing cough made Quinn look up from the latest issue of *Dark Tales,* and he found the hulking figure of Rabbi Shwartz towering over him. Dressed as usual in his bulky black pea coat and heavy boots, he looked more like an intimidating sea captain than a small-town rabbi. Even the town mortician, Mr. Gibbs, never wore so much black.

His eyes were hard and gray as steel, as was his bushy beard and caterpillar sized eyebrows. His hair was a mane of wild gray tangles, as if he were always standing in a powerful wind, or had just stuck a fork inside an electrical socket. He stared down at Quinn with that familiar sneer that made him feel like a bug about to be squashed under a boot.

"What...what can I get you, rabbi?"

Quinn always found himself jumbling his words around Rabbi Shwartz. There was something about the man that left him unsettled. The way he never smiled. How he always dressed in black, even on a sweltering New Hampshire summer day. Or how he didn't seem to talk so much as *growl*, like he'd been gargling with pebbles.

The rabbi tapped on the counter. Two fingers were missing from his right hand, three from his left. The remaining ones were gnarled like twisted roots and thick as ginger husks.

"Haven't seen you at temple lately, Mr. Katz." His voice was deep, and he spoke with a thick German accent.

"No, sir," Quinn said, growing uneasy. The last time he'd been was for his father's funeral. Rabbi Shwartz knew that, of course, and he seemed to enjoy making Quinn feel guilty.

"I trust you're studying your Haftarah." His eyes narrowed. "You *are* planning on celebrating your bar mitzvah this coming year, yes?" He said "celebrate" as if it left a sour taste in his mouth.

"I'm...thinking about it."

The rabbi's eyes darkened. "*Thinking* about it?"

"Henry and me, we don't really...um..."

"Don't really *what*?" he growled.

Quinn felt like the walls were closing in. The truth was, ever since they sat shiva for their father, neither of them much liked the idea of going to temple on Saturdays. Henry stopped going since Ethan died, and Quinn had quit taking Hebrew lessons with Mrs. Epstein two summers ago and hadn't fasted on Yom Kippur since. How could he possibly tell the rabbi that it wasn't...

Important.

That was it, he realized. Since Dad was gone, those things just didn't seem important.

"I'll think about it," Quinn said shakily.

The rabbi let out a small sigh. "You'll be thirteen before you know it. Think harder. And while you're thinking, I'll have a root beer float, please."

Quinn paused. The idea of scary old Rabbi Shwartz, the undertaker of Beth Shalom Synagogue, enjoying a root beer float, of all things, left him dumbstruck.

The fact that he added "please" struck him even more.

"Coming right up."

Something...a hint, maybe, just a hint of a smile spread under that gray beard.

"Thank you," he said, and made his way to the counter. "Jonas!" His gruff voice was suddenly full of cheer.

Like Scrooge at the end of A Christmas Carol, Quinn thought, *when he seems more like a Jacob Marley type.*

The image of the rabbi dragging chains down candlelit hallways sent a cold chill down his back.

Mr. Malman threw out his arms. "Rabbi, good to see you."

"You look well," the rabbi said. "You've been eating?"

Mr. Malman, ever skinny, shrugged. "Much as I can. Appetite is not what it used to be. Not since Ethan…"

"It will pass, Jonas. I know it will."

"A long time, Rabbi…"

"You'll be joining us for our Talmud study? It's just myself and Mrs. Epstein tonight."

"Oh, of course," He put a few more objects into an already bulging paper bag. "Your usual order?"

"Yes." He turned back and met Quinn's eyes. "And a root beer float. I'm in a…*celebratory* mood."

That phrase left Quinn uneasy, though he couldn't figure out why.

"Well, aren't we all," Mr. Malman said. He handed the bag over.

"What do I owe you?"

"Today? Not a penny."

"Nothing? Surely—"

"Rabbi, you've done me one mitzvah after another. I can't repay you enough. Please, take it, free of charge."

Rabbi Shwartz hefted the bag. "You've done me a mitzvah as well. I'll take this and we'll call it even, eh?"

Mr. Malman laughed, nodding. "Can I interest you in a dried apple doll? The proceeds go to fixing the bridge."

The Rabbi eyed the creepy dolls warily. "Mrs. Ruane's doing, I presume? No thank you. I'll pass." He let out a gruff laugh as Mr. Malman made one of the dolls dance on the countertop.

Quinn watched the whole scene play out like he was watching some strange television show. He'd never seen the rabbi so cheerful.

Before he knew it, the huge man was back at the counter.

"I'll take that float, Mr. Katz."

"Sure," Quinn said, sliding the tall cup across the counter. "Made it extra special. Happy Fourth of July, Rabbi. And, uh, shalom." He winced when he said it. *Really?*

Once more, he got the look like the rabbi was deciding which species of bug he was.

"Well...shalom, Quinn. You too."

Quinn let out a sigh of relief as the bells above the door jingled, signaling that he really *had* left.

Hector popped up from his mountain of firework boxes. "You okay?"

"Just fine," Quinn said.

"Look like you saw a *fantasma*." He liked using the Spanish word, and Quinn and Wendy agreed it sounded a whole lot neater than regular old "ghost".

"No fantasma. Just a rabbi."

"Oh, him. He gives me the willies."

"Willies is putting it lightly," Wendy said, also popping up from the firework fort they'd set up.

"Hey, now," Mr. Malman said. "Show some respect. Just because he wears that black coat and talks rough doesn't make him one of those ghouls from those comics you kids like so much. He's a good man."

"Sorry, Mr. Malman," they all said together.

"Oh, and Quinn," he said, "I put a special book on order for you. The latest Stephen King. It's due out soon."

Quinn brightened. "You did? Really?"

"Of course!" Mr. Malman said. "And it's all yours if you make sure to clean the ice cream mixers before you leave." He gave him a wink. "Spotless, eh?"

"Sure thing," Quinn said.

A loud *clang* from the basement made the kids jump.

Mr. Malman threw up his hands. "The boiler," he huffed, "Sometimes I think it breaks on purpose, you know. Just to taunt me."

"You need a hand?" Wendy asked.

"No, no," he said, waving her off. "You kids have been such a help already. How about you give Quinn a hand with those mixers? Leave the boiler to me."

They watched Mr. Malman hitch his overalls and gather his toolbox, disappearing down the dark cellar steps.

The parade began at five o'clock. Quinn, Hector, and Wendy used the ladder and climbed on top of the Malman & Sons sign, their legs dangling over the neon lights as the festivities got underway.

The sidewalks were packed, and it seemed to Quinn that everyone in Stark Falls had come out to celebrate. It was a small town, sure, but 1,100 people all crammed together on a tiny street was nothing to sneeze at, he supposed.

The marching band led the way, followed by the Historical Society, standing on their float dressed up as Revolutionary War soldiers. Then came the Gardening Club, their float looking like something out of a science fiction film, a lurching, gigantic mass of green with tangles of vine and multicolored flowers. Mrs. Ruane sat on top, scowling as she waved to the onlookers below, her ear trumpet decorated with a single daffodil that made her look part plant. Behind them, the Knitting Society riding on a huge ball of yarn, their hair done up with those sharp needles. The local Irish step dancing studio followed, little girls and their instructors twirling and quick stepping to the bagpipes of the Scottish Club. Next was a float with a miniature model of the town, with Calvin Stark, the mayor and patriarch of the ancient (and rich) Stark family, which the town and county were named for. The old man waved, a bit unsteady and teetering on top of the slow-moving float.

Quinn looked down and saw Mr. Malman leaning on the door of the shop, turning the "open" sign to "closed". He smiled, watching the dancers and pipers pass, and suddenly, Quinn could see beneath the neon, his face fell. He took off the coke bottle glasses, and tears welled in his eyes. Quinn watched one fall down his wrinkled cheek. His hands, Quinn noticed with unease, clenched to fists, even as the tears came. Like anger and sadness played tug of war in the old man's head.

Quinn looked back at the parade and saw the line of drummers in their fancy caps and white gloves. Behind them, a huge group of men walked proudly down the street, all wearing their army or navy uniforms, some decorated in medals. He looked back at Mr. Malman, but the old man was gone.

Henry wasn't with his friends. Quinn saw him sitting on the roof of the sheriff's car, parked a few doors down from Malman's. He waved with his hat.

Again, Quinn looked down, wondering what happened to Mr. Malman. It was strange, he thought, him leaving without a goodbye.

The parade went down Main Street at a snail's pace, looping around the green. Once it was over, everyone gathered on the grass, and Mr. Todd's jazz quartet took to the bandstand. While they belted out a snappy version of the Star-Spangled Banner, the fireworks were lit and explosions of red, white and blue burst and bloomed in the sky. The crowd cheered, as did the Crypt Crew, who climbed down the ladder and joined Henry by the car.

Henry was smiling as he looked on at the festivities, but Quinn saw that he flinched with each *bang* and *pop* of the fireworks.

Across the street, a few kids tossed some cherry bombs into a sewer grate, and the resounding bursts caught the new sheriff's attention.

"Hey!" Henry snapped at them in his best lawman's voice. "Cut that out, you hear? I see you, Tom Banores. And you too, Gail Trumbull. Don't think I don't."

The kids took off, disappearing into the crowd on the green.

"So, how's it going?" Quinn asked.

"Yeah, catch any bank robbers today?" Wendy asked.

"Not today, Wen. But there's always hope."

Another firework exploded overhead. Henry's eyes shut tight, his forehead creasing.

"You okay, Sheriff?" Hector asked.

"Yeah, pal. I'm okay. Why don't you guys go have some fun, huh? Can't spend the night hanging around the law, you know. Think I saw Frank Castelot and Terry Pots go off with a couple other kids round back of the hardware store. Your sister, too, Hector." He leaned in, grinning. "Think I saw 'em carrying some pretty fine looking M80s and Atom Blasts."

"Oh, we have some of our ow—"

Quinn elbowed Hector before he could finish.

"That's okay," he told him.

What he really wanted to say was that Frank Castelot and Terry Pots and whoever else they were with would probably use the fireworks on them, just for laughs. But Henry didn't need to know all that. He had enough to deal with.

"I think we'll head back to our place, if that's alright with you. Got a new story to work on."

"Sure. I won't be home until late, so don't burn the place down, will ya?"

"Wouldn't dream of it!" Wendy said.

"I'll radio the clinic and the ranger's office and let your parents know you're at my place, okay? Can't have them thinking I lost three kids in the middle of the town's biggest party of the year."

"Sounds good," Hector said. "Just…don't mention the words "cherry" or "bomb". I kinda want to live to see the *fifth* of July."

Henry gave him a nudge on the shoulder. "My lips are sealed. Be careful riding home."

"We will," Quinn said.

"Hey, guys!"

Abbie Gibbs and Clark Willette made their way through the crowd, their arms loaded with cotton candy. Abbie was the funeral director's daughter. Clark, the Lumber Yard owner's son. Quinn, Hector, and Wendy thought of them as unofficial members of the Crypt Crew, since they seemed to be the only two kids who didn't look at them like they were some kind of science experiment gone wrong.

"Got you these," Abbie said, passing the treats around. "Good thing, too. Mr. Birch is almost sold out."

"Thanks," Quinn said, taking a bite.

"You guys gonna hang around for the movie?" Clark asked. "Mr. Arpin's got the projector from the library. They're gonna show some war movie on the green. I hope it's a good one!"

"Maybe *Rambo*," Hector said hopefully, "or *The Predator*!"

"I don't know if those are the kinds they had in mind," Abbie laughed.

"Wish we could stay and hang," Quinn said, "but we have to go work on this story while the idea's fresh."

"You guys should write a story about Mrs. Ruane's apple dolls," Abbie said. "You see those things?" She shuddered.

"That's what I said!" Wendy laughed.

"Well I hope it's a scary one," Abbie said. "That one about the

Egyptian zombies had me up all night. And the newest one, too. The lizard men were great!"

"*Thank* you," Hector said, puffing up proudly.

"Hey," Clark said between bites of spun sugar, "those are your bikes, right?" He pointed down the street.

Under the darkened neon sign above Malman's, Quinn saw a group of figures huddled around their bikes.

"Hey!" he cried, running towards them. "Hey!"

A loud *pop* rocked Quinn's eardrums followed by a flash of light. He stopped to shield his eyes, and Terry Pots' unmistakable cackle rose over the blast of fireworks. Quinn watched as Maria and Frank lit another Atom Blast, the long wick hissing as the sparking flame slid closer and closer...

Just before the firework went off, Maria shoved it into the spokes of Hector's back wheel.

"Come on!" She said, and before Quinn could reach it in time, they were sprinting around the corner.

Hector's wheel crumpled under the blast, the spokes blackened like Wile-E-Coyote getting a face full of dynamite in the Looney Tunes cartoon. Quinn turned back to the parade, but couldn't spot Henry in the crowd.

"We'll try to find your brother," Abbie said. "Come on, Clark."

"That's alright," Quinn told her. "He's busy enough. We'll..." he turned back to the wreckage, "we'll deal with this."

"I'm sorry," Clark said. "Those guys are rotten."

"Rotten jerks," Abbie muttered.

Hector ran to his bike, which had toppled over onto the sidewalk. He knelt down, inspecting the damage.

"I'm telling Mom!" he yelled. "You hear me, Maria?"

Wendy knelt beside him.

"Come on," she said. "It's not worth it. We'll walk, okay?"

Hector nodded, sniffling.

"It'll be alright," she said.

"Yeah," Quinn agreed. "I think Henry has a few spare wheels in the garage. We'll fix yours up tonight."

"We'll let Henry know what happened," Abbie said, pulling Clark along, his face still covered with cotton candy.

Hector turned away. Quinn could see him try to wipe away the tears from his eyes as quickly as he could.

Quinn and Wendy took their bikes off the kickstands while Hector lifted his up, testing the back wheel, which was more square than circle, now. He swung his leg over the side and tried to pedal, but the wheel wouldn't budge. Finally, he resigned himself to pushing it.

Quinn stood for a moment watching him, suddenly furious at Maria.

"Quinn, you coming? I've been dying to tell you guys my new idea."

"Coming," Quinn said.

Above them, the sign reading "MALMAN" went dark. As they pedaled down the confetti-covered street, "SON'S" followed, buzzing loudly before blinking out into darkness.

The streets were quiet with everyone still at the celebration, and the Crypt Crew liked that just fine. They walked their bikes at a slow pace. The dark, empty roads made for great storytelling, and Hector had a good one. His mood had lifted the further they walked from the center of town, and now that it was just the three of them, he leapt into his story.

"The duendes," he said, "Are an old folktale from Spain, one that my abuela learned when she was a girl in Mexico. They live in the walls of children's bedrooms, and snip off their toenails if they don't take enough baths!" He paused, waiting for their reactions.

Quinn had to stop himself from laughing. He looked over and saw Wendy doing the same.

"They're, what, little groomers?" she asked.

Hector's cheeks reddened. "No," he said emphatically, "they're evil little gnomes that spy on kids who don't follow the rules. The toenails are just a part of it. Isn't that creepy? Abuela used to tell me that if I didn't scrub under my nails enough, they'd come for me. She also made me stop chewing on them. They get you for that, too."

Quinn couldn't help himself anymore and burst out laughing.

"So they're like the tooth fairy," he said, "but for clean nails."

"Nail fairies," Wendy said.

"Hey, I'm just telling *you* what abuela told *me*," Hector said. "Sure kept me up nights, wondering if I did a good enough job in the tub. She said they know when you don't wash behind your ears, too. And I've washed behind mine ever since."

"I always said the back of your ears sparkle," Wendy said.

"Yeah, yeah, laugh it up," Hector said. "The duendes seem harmless, but that's the point. The really scary thing is that sometimes they clip too much, and take a toe or a finger with them. To *eat*."

The Crypt Crew rode in silence for a few moments to dwell on that.

"Flesh eating creatures that live in walls," Quinn said, thinking. "We can do something with that."

"Maybe change the not washing behind the ears part," Wendy suggested. "And skip the whole clipping business. Why don't they just eat parts of the kids? That would make it a lot scarier."

"And it can be set in an orphanage," Quinn suggested. "That way there's a lot more victims."

"Yeah!" Hector said. "And maybe once a few too many kids get eaten, the other orphans start to wise up. Maybe they go looking for the things making all those sounds in the walls."

"Hector, that's it!" Wendy said. "*The Sound in the Walls*. That could be our title."

"I like it. Sounds like an Edgar Allen Poe story. Quinn?"

"Sounds good to me," Quinn said. He was thinking about something a little catchier, like *Night of the Blood Drinking Gnomes*, but he liked Wendy's idea. It was fancier, and would probably look better in a magazine. She always came up with the best names for their stories.

They walked down Carpenter Place, nearing Quinn's house. As Hector and Wendy spit-balled how she should draw the duendes, Quinn stopped.

Wendy and Hector ground to a halt just ahead of him.

"What's wrong?"

Quinn pointed to the small white house across the street.

Wendy peered across the street. "That's Randall Colburn's place, right? Henry's friend?"

"And Maria's summer school teacher," Hector added.

Quinn nodded. It was Randall's place, all right. But he wondered just what on earth had happened.

For starters, the whole house was lit up like a Christmas tree. Strange, considering the entire neighborhood was pitch dark, with everyone still down at the firework show. But having all the lights on wasn't what stopped Quinn in his tracks.

The front door was busted open, every window shattered.

Quinn could see the broken shards glittering just under the panes.

Broken from the inside out, Quinn noted.

"No way," Hector said in a tight voice, "Mr. Colburn's been robbed!"

"We should get your brother," Wendy said.

"Maybe he got into a fight with someone?" Hector mused.

"He lives alone," Quinn said.

"I still vote for getting your brother," Wendy insisted.

Quinn considered that.

We should, he thought. But what if Randall was hurt? It would take a while to get back to the center of town. Even longer to find Henry in the crowd. By the time they got back, it might be too late.

One step at a time, he told himself. *You don't even know if he's in there.*

"I think...I think we should check it out."

"What?" Hector hissed.

"He might be in trouble," Quinn said. "And if he is, we can use his phone to call the station."

"Quinn, I don't know," Wendy said. "This looks bad. Like..." She lowered her voice, "*violent* bad."

"*Murder* bad," Hector agreed.

Quinn walked his bike over to the sidewalk, gently setting it against the tree by Mr. Colburn's mailbox. Eyes trained on the broken-down front door, he crept across the lawn, making sure to stay alongside the row of hedges, where there was at least some shadow cover.

He neared the entrance, looking for any sign of movement. He strained his ears. Faintly, very faintly, he could hear music. It sounded off, like it was coming from underwater, all slow and warped. He listened for voices, for shouts and screams. Aside from the weird music, there was nothing.

He turned back and motioned for Hector and Wendy to come

closer. They glanced at each other, then at the house, until Wendy nodded and put her bike next to Quinn's.

Hector followed, though Quinn could clearly see this wasn't going to be his night. He struggled to keep up, awkwardly running across the front lawn in a zigzag pattern until he did a barrel roll that nearly knocked Quinn into the hedges.

"Sorry," Hector said, holding Quinn steady. "Can't be too careful. The murderer might be inside, waiting for his next victim to come walking by. We have to be coy, you know. Like spies in the movies."

"I don't think there's anyone in there," Quinn said. "Listen."

"What's that music?" Wendy asked.

Hector and Quinn shook their heads.

"The sound in the walls," Hector muttered.

"I don't think we're dealing with duendes, here," Wendy said.

"No, of course not," Hector agreed. "Just a maniac with a knife. Colburn's probably in pieces. Sliced and diced. All that blood..." Hector shook himself, his cheeks losing their color.

"Don't talk like that," Quinn said. "Let's check it out."

"Check it out?! Look, I like spooky stuff just as much as you, but this is real life. And that's different, in case you didn't know. *Way* different. I'm not getting hacked to bits by some mask-wearing psycho. We can't just write our way out of this if it goes bad."

"No," Quinn said, "we can't. But we're the only ones on this street. The only ones on this whole block. We have to at least look."

"Okay," Wendy said. "I'm in."

"Well, this is just *great*," Hector said. "Real great, Quinn. You know, I wasn't kidding when I told Henry I'd like to live to see the *fifth* of July. Guess I really put my foot in my mouth, huh?"

"Come on," Quinn said. "The Crypt Crew sticks together, right?"

"Through thick and thin," Wendy agreed.

"Can't I keep watch here? I'll give you guys a signal. I'll yodel. Or bark like a dog."

"You can yodel all you want," Wendy told him. "Inside with us. Quinn, you lead the way."

Quinn's sneakers crunched on broken glass. The door wasn't just kicked in. It was lying in the entryway in pieces, shredded.

He took the first step into the house, and a queasy feeling churned in his belly. Something was wrong. Very wrong. The warped music only added to the nightmare that was Randall Colburn's living room.

Everything was covered in mud. At least Quinn thought it was mud. It was splashed against the wallpaper, dripping from parts of the ceiling, globs of it hanging like stalactites in the roof of a cave. Quinn walked a bit further in and saw that Randall's couch had been toppled over, along with every other piece of furniture, some of which was just as splintered and shredded as the door. Mud oozed off everything.

Quinn crouched down near a big glob of the stuff. It was reddish brown.

"Don't touch it!" Hector said. "It might be radioactive."

"I don't think so," Wendy said. "It'd be glowing, wouldn't it?"

"Yeah," Hector said, "like in *Invasion of the Astro Men*."

Just to be sure, Quinn grabbed a piece of splintered wood and prodded it. It felt like wet cement. And it stank. The smell reminded him of a moldy, wet cellar.

"Look at these," Wendy said, pointing to the carpet.

"Those can't be real," Hector said.

Quinn looked down and saw footprints. *Enormous* footprints. Quinn had seen clowns at the carnival when it passed through Nashua two years before, and their shoes were the biggest he'd ever seen. But these were twice that. He scratched his head, wondering what size that would even be. Twenty? Twenty-five?

The muddy footprints were everywhere. Whoever left them must have been a giant.

There are no giants, he told himself. *No beanstalks that shoot up past the clouds.*

Those things were all well and good in the pages of a book. But not for real. Real life was different. Hector was right on that count. There were no giants or mud monsters or gnomes living in walls. No dream-stalking killers with knives for hands, or shape-shifting aliens snatching people for their experiments.

Not in Stark Falls, New Hampshire, at least.

They explored the other rooms. Each one was the same. Broken furniture and globs of muddy goop. Dripping. Oozing.

"They go this way," Wendy said, following the tracks.

In the kitchen, they found the source of the music. A record player was set up next to the counter. Like everything else, it was splattered, so the music was playing at a slowed speed.

It was a record by the Midnight Crooners, a singing group that was popular when Quinn's dad was his age. Weird that Randall had such old taste in music. He would have expected Van Halen. Maybe The Cars or the B-52's.

The song was an old standard called "Glow Worm". Quinn knew it by heart, but the way it came all slow and garbled out of the gunky speaker made his skin crawl, and the normally sweet voices of the Crooners sounded like a chorus of demons.

"Whoever did this, I think they're gone," Hector said, pointing to the door at the far end of the kitchen. Or where the door used to be. It lay outside in the grass. Whoever knocked it down had done it from the inside going out.

Quinn turned back to the record player. It wasn't just the voices that scared him. Whoever did this to Randall's house had been there just minutes before they rode by. He picked up the record sleeve and looked at the track list. "Glow Worm" was the fourth song. He looked at the song lengths of the previous tracks. The queasy sensation filled his belly again.

"Seven minutes," he said softly. "We missed him by seven minutes."

Wendy raced over to the phone on the wall.

"It works," she said after slicking the wet clay from the cord. "I'll call the station."

Once the call was made, they stood in Randall Colburn's kitchen, listening as the demonic voices garbled out the last lines of the song.

"*Shine, little glow-worm, glimmer*
Shine, little glow-worm, glimmerrrrrrrrrr"

The record ground to a halt as the needle snapped and the kitchen fell into an eerie silence.

A Strange Case

It wasn't long before Deputy Henry arrived with Dale Francis, Wendy's dad, the Stark County forest ranger. He was, Quinn guessed, the closest thing a deputy had to a partner in town.

They turned the place upside down, looking for any sign of Randall. The Crypt Crew waited in the kitchen while the adults conducted their search.

"Strange," Henry said when they finished their rounds of the house. "No blood. Could be some vandal just came and messed the place up." He frowned. "Maybe Randall did it himself, but I can't see that."

"Did you see him at the fireworks?" Quinn asked.

Henry shook his head. "In that crowd? No."

"So he could have been here when this...stuff happened. He could have been taken by whoever did it."

Henry nodded. "He could have. And it worries me, Q. Worries me big time."

Quinn knew Randall. One of Henry's best friends, a big guy, almost as big as Rabbi Shwartz. And tough. He was the Stark Falls High football coach. Quinn had a hard time imagining anyone giving Randall physical trouble. Let alone kidnapping him from his own house.

Mr. Francis entered the kitchen from the backyard, flashlight in hand.

"Prints go out a few paces and just vanish," He said. "Like someone took off into the sky."

"Space invaders," Hector whispered.

"Same out front," Henry said. Quinn heard the frustration in his brother's voice.

"You kids stay put," Henry said, "Let Mr. Francis and I have another look around."

They did, but that didn't stop them from eavesdropping at the doorway.

"Can't wrap my head around it," Quinn heard Henry saying.

"Strange as all get out, and no mistake," Mr. Francis replied.

Quinn watched as they crouched down in the hallway, examining one of the muddy footprints.

"What do you suppose made these?" Henry asked. "No foot is this big, unless we're dealing with a record breaker, here."

Mr. Francis measured the length of the print with his hands.

"You ever been snowshoeing, Henry?"

"Can't say I have. Sledding and skiing, sure."

"Some folks use them to get out to their ice fishing huts, or up the mountains past the falls where the good hunting is. These prints are too big for a sneaker or a loafer. But a snowshoe? Maybe."

"You'd know better than me," Henry said.

Mr. Francis stood up, wiping some of the mud from his hands.

"Just a theory."

"And it would be hard, I'm guessing, for someone to do all this mess with a huge pair of wooden contraptions tied to their feet."

"They're not easy to walk in, no. Even a grizzled woodsman would be stumbling around, wearing them in July."

"Bringing me to my next question. This...stuff all over. This mud."

"Clay," Mr. Francis said. "Wet clay, but that doesn't make a bit of sense. Hasn't rained in a week. River's more than a mile away. And even if it did, how did so much get from a clay bed to this house without leaving it all over the street?"

"The intruder brought it," Henry suggested. "Loaded up a truck with bags of the stuff, then threw it around."

"Would've been a lot," Mr. Francis said. "We're talking huge amounts. No one could carry that much. The bags would weigh close to a few hundred pounds. Then to step in it? Wet it down and haul it in here with snowshoes on? For what?"

"To confuse us? They've done a good job, so far."

"Of course!"

The two looked to Wendy, whose eyes lit up as realization dawned.

"That clay," she said, "It's like the stuff we use in art class. Only... bad. Wrong, somehow."

"Who'd have something like that?" Henry asked, removing a small notepad from his shirt pocket.

"School teacher, for one. Or an artist. Like a sculptor. I got some for my birthday a while back, remember?"

"Um," Mr. Francis said, scratching the back of his head. "Which one was that?"

Wendy's jaw clenched. Quinn could hear her teeth grinding.

"We went to the art supply store in Manchester. Took the trip down, just you and me."

Mr. Francis clapped his hands. "Oh! Yes! Of course, honey. That was a nice day. Your tenth birthday!"

"Ninth," Wendy muttered under her breath.

"Art teacher. Sculptor," Henry said, writing quickly. He turned to Mr. Francis. "Mason, you think?"

Dale shrugged. "Jacques Arpin is the only mason I know of, and I don't think they use clay."

Quinn thought about Mrs. Gussen, the Stark Falls junior high art teacher. He had a hard time picturing her bashing down Randall Colburn's door, given how she was in a wheelchair and almost eighty.

Mr. Francis looked back at the footprint. "Henry, you sure you're up for this?"

"I am," he said after a moment.

"Alright. Then I'm with you. I know Randall was your pal. We'll figure this mess out."

"Thanks, Dale."

"Anyone you can think of that'd have a grudge against him?"

"Well," Henry said, "He's taken on the job of being the county elementary summer school teacher. I could list off a few kids who'd be happy to see him go."

"Yikes. You don't think..."

"No," Henry said quickly, waving it off. "Just thinking out loud. Wasn't a bunch of kids who did this. At least I don't believe it."

Quinn made sure to look busy when they came back into the kitchen, pretending to study the Midnight Crooners record.

Like he hadn't just heard the sheriff and the park ranger admit they had no clue what was going on.

That scared him more than anything.

"Odd," Henry said as he studied the record. "Randall hated this sort of stuff."

"Alright," Mr. Francis said to Wendy. "I think it's time I took you home. You too, Hector. Why don't you kids go load your bikes in the truck."

"Tire's busted," Hector said.

"I'll drop one off tomorrow," Henry told him.

Quinn watched Wendy and Hector follow Mr. Francis through the clay-covered hallway and out to the truck. They looked tired. And scared.

And it was his fault, for getting them into this mess.

You had to come inside, didn't you? Just had to check it out. Couldn't keep on riding.

He kicked himself, then stopped. Randall was Henry's friend. And if the situation were reversed, Quinn hoped someone would come looking for him if he ever got attacked by a maniac wearing snowshoes and slinging clay.

He paused, that bizarre image in his head. Was that *really* what they think happened? Neither Henry nor Mr. Francis seemed too keen on it.

"Doesn't make sense," he said.

"No," Henry said from the other side of the kitchen, "It sure doesn't."

"What do we do now?"

Henry looked lost in thought, hand idly fiddling with the badge on his chest.

"Now, I think I should get you home. Doesn't look like I'm going to sleep any time soon. I'll call a few friends, get a search party going. If Randall has been snatched, hopefully his snatcher hasn't gotten too far." He tapped his notepad. "I have a few people I need to question, too."

Quinn nodded, thinking of a giant in snowshoes trampling through the woods behind Randall's house, covered in wet, moldy clay. He didn't think he'd get to sleep any time soon, either.

Quinn spent the better part of the night idly flipping through comics, trying to figure out just what it was they'd stumbled upon at Randall Colburn's. The more he read from *Tales From the Crypt* and *Horror Haunts*, the more his mind drifted to the image he'd concocted in Randall's kitchen.

A giant covered in clay. Snowshoes strapped to its feet.

Hector's story about the duendes entered his mind, and he pictured the giant bursting from the walls, hungry for Randall Colburn's limbs.

"Get a grip," he told himself, and put the comics back in the pile. His father always said that reading those things would sour his mind, but Quinn always found an odd sense of comfort in them. Maybe it was knowing that whatever horrors he found on the page would never come into his own world. They could stay right there, and he could close the cover any time.

Quinn knew that there were plenty of things in the real world that were far scarier than anything the Crypt Keeper or monster movies could dish out. Henry had seen real horror when he lost Ethan Malman on Stark River. Mr. Malman had felt it when his son never came home. He could fill a small notebook with the names of all the folks in Stark Falls who'd been shipped off to fight in Vietnam, and all the wars before that.

There were other horrors, too. Things like car crashes, which got his mother when Quinn was only three. Cancer, which took his dad. Racism and ignorance, which he saw Hector deal with, and Wendy, too, just because her folks were divorced. Kids said the nastiest things about her mother, especially. They said nasty things about Quinn, too, because he was Jewish. Stark Falls was a small town, where everyone knew everyone and waved and smiled, but that didn't stop a few rotten eggs from soaping Malman's storefront or Rabbi Shwartz's synagogue with mean symbols and bad words. He'd caught Terry Pots and Frank Castelot trying to break Malman's windows, once. Another time they were drawing on them in soap; big Stars of David that streaked across the whole storefront. Sheriff Toohey had seen them and dragged each boy home by the ear. Even so, they laughed.

Those were the scary things. How cruel people could be. Atom bombs. Hiding under their desks during nuclear drills, just in case the Russians decided to drop the big one.

Compared to the real world, the stories Quinn, Hector, and Wendy wrote were fun. It was how they escaped, he figured. How they coped with a world filled with bad things, filled with people who liked being mean for mean's sake.

With a world like that, why shouldn't there be a kidnapping giant covered in clay, stomping around on snowshoes with Randall Colburn's fingers and toes?

"Quinn?"

He was so lost in thought he hadn't heard Henry pull into the driveway.

Quinn met Henry in the living room. He was joined by Martin Ward. Martin gave Quinn a tired wave, resting his bulky frame on his cane. Like Henry, he had lingering afflictions from the day on the river. He'd been there when Ethan died, and like Henry, he'd done everything he could to save him, including almost losing a leg.

"Anything?"

"Not yet," Henry said.

Martin plopped down on the couch. "Henry told me about you walking into Randall's. That took guts, little Katz." The big man grinned.

"Martin's gonna stay over here tonight," Henry said. "We'll get a fresh start at dawn."

"You guys think he's, you know—" Quinn stopped himself. Henry bristled. Martin shifted uncomfortably on the couch.

The unspoken word hung in the air.

Gone.

And worse, *dead*.

"I hope not, Q. I really do."

"Just wouldn't be right," Martin said quietly. "First Ethan, now Randall..."

"Come on, now," Henry said. "For all we know, he could have had a bad night. Gotten into a fight with someone, lost his temper, skipped out. We just don't know."

Martin considered that. "You ever know Randall to lose his cool?"

"No," Henry said. "But that doesn't mean it can't happen."

"Some kind of maniac on the loose," Martin said. "Doesn't make any sense."

"No, it doesn't," Henry said as he turned to Quinn, "And speaking of, no more rushing into ransacked houses, okay? Next time—and I hope there isn't a next time—you find me or ring Mabel at the station."

Henry was starting to get dark circles under his eyes. Quinn was worried that this whole business would bring back his nightmares even worse than before. But he wasn't going to say that in front of Martin. He probably had them, too.

"You should try to catch some winks," Quinn said, trying to smile. "Our town needs its Sheriff rested and ready."

Now, more than ever.

"We'll be searching from sunup to sundown, maybe longer," Henry said. "I know you like helping out at Malman's, but tomorrow I want you here with the door locked." He held up a hand, "I'm not grounding you," he said. "I just want to make sure I know where you are."

"If I went to Malman's you'd know where I was."

Henry gave a tired smile. "Quinn, do this for me, please? Work on one of your stories. Read some comics. Catch a scary flick on television. Just one day."

"Alright," Quinn said. He had some books he was planning on reading during the school year but never got around to. Maybe they would take his mind off of things.

He went back to his room, opening up *I Am Legend* by Richard Matheson. The book was about the last mortal man in a world full of vampires. Quinn was hooked from the first page and read it all night and into the morning.

He made coffee for Henry and Martin, wished them good luck, and then sat at his desk and painted his Godzilla model kit, the newest one that Malman had gotten at the store, which led him into the late afternoon.

After dinner, Quinn slid a plastic tub from under his bed and sifted through the comics and books until he came across a stack of newspapers. He held up the first one, which read "Local Heroes Save Nature Scout Troop". There was a photo of Henry, Martin, Randall, and Brent Foster standing behind a group of kids, the river at their backs. But no Ethan. Quinn knew that thirteen kids would have died in the rapids that day had Henry and the rest not been close by. They were heroes, and the town remembered. Quinn didn't doubt that it helped Henry get elected as Deputy.

It was past midnight, and with no phone call from Henry, he fell asleep watching *Taste the Blood of Dracula* on *Nightmare Theater*.

In his dreams, a clay-covered giant with the face of Randall Colburn chased him through a dark forest while a murder of skeleton crows shrieked a chilling rendition of "Glow Worm" from the pines, worms wriggling helplessly in their decaying beaks.

Quinn was happy to be back at Malman's the next day, but the mood was different than it had been on the Fourth. A lot had happened in two days. The morning crowd entered, all hushes and whispers. No small talk. No jokes. Quinn watched as everyone came in, grabbed what they needed, and left in a hurry.

The Falls were on edge.

Henry's search party had come up with nothing, and everyone he questioned (including old Mrs. Gussen) had been at the fireworks on the Fourth.

"Terrible. Just terrible," Mr. Malman said, putting down the paper.

Quinn read the headline:

Snowshoe Snatcher Eludes Search! Will He Strike Again?
  Rookie Deputy Starts Case on Shaky Footing

Malman shook his head ruefully. "Let's just hope Randall turns up safe and sound."

The Crypt Crew was seated around the soda counter, joined by Abbie and Clark. Wendy was hunched over a large sheet of paper, a paintbrush dancing like magic in her hand. Hector had planted himself in front of Donkey Kong, listening while furiously toggling the joystick.

"That story has my Dad all worked up," Clark said. "He said a bunch of the guys at the Yard are taking bets on who the Snatcher is."

"Taking bets?" Abbie asked. "That's awful."

Clark shrugged. "Not much else to do when you're choppin' away." He leaned over Wendy's shoulder, watching as she touched up the picture with bits of red and brown.

"What is that thing?" He pointed to the creature lurking beneath an untidy bed, red eyes bulging from its thin, yellow face.

"A duende," Wendy said. "For our next story."

"Looks good," Clark said.

"You should've seen it," Hector said, acting out their discovery at Mr. Colburn's house. "There was this stuff everywhere, this—"

"Hector," Wendy said, "we're not supposed to talk about it."

"What, not even to them?" He jerked his thumb toward Abbie and Clark.

Wendy motioned to the handful of customers roaming around the store. Mrs. Ruane was pretending to look at a tin of cat food, glancing back at them with narrowed eyes, one hand adjusting her ear trumpet in their direction.

"She'd make a terrible spy," Quinn whispered to Abbie, who let out a snort.

"Because it's an ongoing case," Wendy said, "My Dad said you're not supposed to give out details."

"Well how can I not?" he said. "The details are just so...so..."

"Frightening," Mr. Malman finished for him. "I think Wendy's right. Maybe this isn't the best talk for the customers to be hearing."

He nodded to Mrs. Ruane. "Still trying to sell those dolls!"

Mrs. Ruane let out an indignant huff, clearly embarrassed to be caught eavesdropping, and shuffled further down the aisle.

"What a shame," he continued. "Hector, why don't you turn on the radio? We need some music this morning, and I like that Madman fellow."

"I still can't believe you guys actually went inside Mr. Colburn's house," Abbie said.

"Seriously," Clark said. "That took guts."

"Yeah, well," Hector said, squaring his shoulders. "Someone had to do it."

"And *someone* wanted to wait outside and bark like a dog," Wendy added, elbowing him.

Hector stepped away from the machine. "Hey! New high score!"

Quinn looked at the screen, which asked Hector to put in his 3 initials. But the number one spot read EJM. Ethan Judah Malman. Hector saw, too, and decided to not enter in his own name.

"He should keep it," Quinn heard him say. "He did good."

The smoky voice of Rick "Madman" Wade echoed through the store, wishing everyone a good morning as "Everybody Wants to Rule the World" by Tears for Fears played.

Quinn went behind the soda counter. He took a deep breath to calm himself and poured a Pepsi, waiting for the fizz to settle before taking a big gulp.

"Mr. Katz."

The voice snapped him from his thoughts. Soda dribbled down his chin. He looked up and saw—

A clay-covered giant in snowshoes!

Quinn shook his head, running a hand over his face.

Rabbi Shwartz stared down at him.

"Did I wake you?"

"No, rabbi. Just—"

"Daydreaming," The rabbi said. "Ever the daydreamer, eh, Quinn? I'll take another root beer float."

Quinn paused, his hands hovering over the handle of the ice cream machine.

"I know," the rabbi said, as if reading his thoughts. "Three mornings in a row. Hector made a delicious one for me yesterday. So much ice cream can't be good for the stomach. But these have been trying times. I hear you were the one who found that mess at Randall Colburn's."

"Me, Hector, and Wendy," Quinn said.

"Hector, Wendy, and *I*," the rabbi corrected.

"Yes, sir."

Rabbi Shwartz drummed his large hands on the counter. "Randall Colburn. He was Jewish on his mother's side. Did you know that? He was always a good student in Hebrew school. Never missed temple on the Sabbath. Always singing. Marvelous voice. I wanted him to be Beth Shalom's permanent cantor, you know." He eyed Quinn. "One could learn from such a fine example."

Quinn felt his cheeks go red. He poured in the soda, but when he went to pass over the glass it slipped from his hands, showering the floor with soda and globs of vanilla ice cream.

The rabbi launched himself around the counter. He grabbed a sheet of paper towels and bent down to help him sop up the mess.

"I apologize," he said, "for distracting you."

"It's okay," Quinn said, sloshing the sticky mixture along the tile floor.

"I suppose I'm hard on you," the rabbi said, his gruff voice very low. "But it's because I care. For your father and mother's sake. I really hope you think on your bar mitzvah. They would have wanted that for you."

Quinn looked up at the rabbi, and for the first time in a long time, didn't get the sense that the imposing man was berating or judging him. He was sincere.

"Thanks, rabbi," he said, trying to mask his surprise. "I'll…I'll think about it. Really."

Rabbi Shwartz grunted and stood. "Good boy."

When he turned to face the counter, Quinn froze.

The sides of his pants and coat were covered in red, chalky stains.

The rabbi looked down at Quinn, patting the leg of his pants.

"I really should take these to the cleaners."

"Is that…clay?" Quinn held his breath, pulse pounding in his ears as the rabbi cocked his head curiously.

"Clay?" he asked, bewildered. "No. Brick dust. I've been doing some masonry at the synagogue to fix those pesky back steps." He brushed the smudges off the sleeve of his coat. "I had to miss the fireworks because of it. A shame. I was really looking forward to it. I'll take you up on a root beer float some other time," he said, and then waved to Mr. Malman.

Quinn watched the rabbi walk away, staring at the reddish-brown marks all down the back of his coat, and thought of a giant in snowshoes.

"Jonas," the rabbi said, gripping Mr. Malman's shoulder, "it was so good to see you last night."

Quinn did his best to not look like he was eavesdropping.

"You too, rabbi. You were a big help. It's been...difficult. Harder lately than it was in the beginning, actually."

"And what do I always say? Hm? It will get better. Time heals, Jonas. You will come to see that."

"Yes," Mr. Malman said.

Quinn saw a glint of sadness in his eyes. Mr. Malman's shoulders slumped.

"You can call on me any time," the rabbi said. "I have some books which might interest you. Things that can be of use."

"Thank you. I will."

"Good," Rabbi Shwartz said and clapped him on the shoulder once more.

As he did, another loud *bang* echoed up from the basement.

"That boiler," Mr. Malman sighed, "will be the death of me. Please excuse me, rabbi. Thing's been on the fritz these past few days."

The bells jangled over the door as Hampton Harwich, the owner, editor in chief, and principal writer of *The Stark Falls Minuteman*, the town's only newspaper, walked in. The small, moleish man was grinning so wide he looked like a jack o'lantern.

"Well!" he said, gesturing to the stack of Minuteman issues. "Finally something that'll put this town on the map!" He rubbed his hands together. "Exciting, no?"

"Yeah," Wendy said, "if you want to give everyone in Stark Falls a heart attack."

Harwich frowned. "Ms. Francis, I'll have you know that *this* is what sells." He lifted a copy and waved it in front of her face. "Blood sells. The real gushy stuff."

"Mr. Harwich." The rabbi loomed behind him. "This is neither the time nor the place to be boasting about your journalistic accomplishments." He nodded subtly to Mr. Malman, who was standing downcast at the counter. "Perhaps you should purchase what you need and go brag somewhere else, hm? I'm sure there's someone who'd love to chat with you about all that...gushy stuff."

Harwich's face scrunched into a mess of angry wrinkles.

"Well," he huffed, "if that's the opinion of those present, I'll take my business elsewhere." He spun on the heels of his loafers and made for the exit.

"Foolish," Quinn heard the rabbi mutter under his breath. "I'll buy the whole stack just to drop it in the trash."

It was a few minutes before Mr. Malman had gathered himself. He stopped before he reached the basement door. "Oh, kids! Your sandwiches are ready." He glanced down at his watch. "You've been a big help, as ever. I'll be fine on my own for a while." He paused on the first step. "Wendy, I made an extra sandwich there for your father. Why don't you kids head up there and surprise him with some lunch?"

"Sure, Mr. Malman."

"Sounds good to me!" Hector said, resting the broom against the wall.

Quinn cleaned up the last traces of the spill. When he finished, Wendy and Hector were ready, brown paper bags in hand.

"Let's head out," Wendy said. "Maybe Dad can give us a good scoop on our Snowshoe Snatcher."

Quinn felt another shiver.

Was it brick dust?

"I think," he said quietly, "I have a scoop of my own."

"Careful," the rabbi said behind them. "'He who hunts monsters must take care to not become a monster himself'." He smiled tiredly. "A saying, but one I've found to be true."

Quinn stared at the large man for a moment before awkwardly backing out of the store, feeling Shwartz's eyes on him the whole time.

The Crypt Crew rode their bikes up Main Street and onto Hodges Road, passing by the Castelot's Textile mill. It was a sprawling place. Nearly half the town worked there, while the other worked at Willette's Lumber Yard.

Quinn waited until they had left downtown before he told them what he saw.

"Rabbi Shwartz?" Hector said, stunned. "Seriously?"

"That's what I saw. I don't know if it means anything or not, but he was covered in the stuff."

"He said it was brick," Wendy said, face furrowed in thought. "But dried clay leaves that same sort of dust. Like chalk."

"You guys," Hector said, huffing as they rode up the narrow road alongside Stark River, "He's scary, sure. But we've known him all our lives. And now all of a sudden he decides to become a kidnapper? Maybe he really was fixing the steps."

"At night?" Quinn asked.

"Why not?" Hector said. "Mr. Bergeron across the street waters his lawn at midnight. Says it's better for the grass. People do weird things."

"Anything's possible," Wendy said. "And he's big enough to fit the description. He ever mention snowshoeing?"

They passed the gates of Fall's Rest cemetery. Quinn looked between the iron bars and saw the rows of stones. A cold feeling passed over him. He usually loved the cemetery. It was spooky in all the right ways. Now it seemed a bit more... sinister.

That's where he takes them, he thought. *The giant. That's where Randall will end up.*

"Well I don't like it," Hector said. "Why don't we take a break for a while. Maybe work on that story about the duendes. *The Sound in the Walls*. You come up with a good plot yet, guys?"

Quinn would have liked nothing more than to sit and write another story, but he'd read three books in a row, and today the real life mystery of the Snowshoe Snatcher consumed his thoughts.

"Sorry, no," he said. "We will though. Let's go over it again at the Falls."

The road grew narrow as it twisted through the forested hills outside of town. A quarter mile in, the pavement turned to gravel, shadowed by pine trees. A wooden sign announcing "**STARK FALLS STATE PARK**" greeted them.

"Hey," Wendy said, "Is that what I think it is?"

Something large was on the side of the road, but the shadow beneath the pines made it hard to see clearly.

The Crypt Crew slowed as they approached.

It was a car, turned upside down in a ditch. Quinn pedaled slower. He'd know that car anywhere. A DeLorean. Quinn had wanted one ever since he saw the commercial for that new *Back to the Future* movie.

"That's Martin Ward's car!"

When he was close enough, Quinn leapt from his bike and ran over to the car, shoes skidding along the gravel road.

Martin's car looked like it had been smashed by a wrecking ball. The entire left side was caved in. Two wheels were ripped clean off, deflated and tossed a few feet away. Quinn crouched down, peering through the shattered windows, bracing himself for the worst.

There was no one inside. Only Martin's cane, broken in half.

"Quinn! You should see this."

Quinn picked himself up, careful not to step on the glass from the broken windshield.

What he saw turned his legs to jelly.

It looked like giant claws had shredded the metal right off the doors. Huge, jagged gouges ran through the panels and into the seat cushions.

"What could have made those?"

"I don't know," Quinn said. "A bear?"

"No way," Hector said. "Dinosaur, more like. T-Rex." He spread out his hands. "We're talking huge. Like the nasty one in *King Kong* huge."

Whatever it was, Quinn knew it was big. Big and *mean*.

The gouges weren't the only thing wrong.

Everywhere they looked, there was clay.

Red and brown, splattered all over the car.

Quinn saw the footprints, then. They circled the car, the same long strides, the same enormous shoes. He followed them until they disappeared into the woods. There were other marks in the clay, too. Chunks torn up. Handprints and gashes from fingernails, like scratches on the surface of a chalkboard.

"He was dragged through," Quinn said, imagining poor Martin struggling in all that muck.

"Dragged," Wendy echoed, "and trying to claw his way out."

"Wendy," Hector said, slowly backing away, "I think we should go find your dad."

"And what's this?" A voice shouted from up the path.

Terry Pots, Frank Castelot, and Maria stepped out from the woods and onto the dirt road. Terry and Frank were in their Nature Scout getups. Maria followed behind, still in her regular school clothes. Terry led them closer, pausing as his eyes fell on Martin's car.

"Hey," Hector called to his sister, "shouldn't you be in summer school?"

She scowled at him. "We got a day off. That's what happens when your teacher goes missing, doofus. Old Mrs. Gussen starts tomorrow. If she doesn't croak first."

Quinn could see Hector's cheeks going tomato red and he stepped between them. "Terry, did you see or hear anything suspicious around here?"

Terry shook his head, attention fixed on the wreck.

"We...we just got back from our first Scout meeting."

Quinn realized it was the first time he'd ever asked Terry a question without getting some snide remark in return. It felt strange.

"Yeah," Frank said, sounding very far away. "Testing our compass skills..." He took a few tentative steps towards the car. Terry and Maria followed close behind. They rounded the wreck, muttering amongst themselves as they took in the damage.

"What happened here?" Terry asked.

"Your guess is as good as ours," Wendy said.

"Sure," Frank said. "This is the second crime scene you three just happened to stumble upon?"

"I don't believe it," Terry said, "not for a minute."

"Whoa," Wendy said, taking a step toward him. "You think we had something to do with this?"

"Gee, Wendy, let me think...aside from us, you three are the only ones around for miles."

"And you think we're strong enough to crush a *car*?" Quinn asked.

"As if," Wendy sneered.

"But still," Maria said, "why do you always find this stuff? Are you guys some kind of tragedy magnet?"

"Maybe they're cursed," Frank said. "Messing around with too many Ouija boards or whatever."

"Oh, *brilliant* idea," Wendy said.

"Cursed with bad looks, maybe," Terry said.

"Go pound sand, Pots," Wendy shot back.

"Yeah? Make me."

"Enough!" Quinn said. "Look, guys, we just got here. We don't know who or what did this, but we have to get to the station so Mr. Francis can call my brother."

"Deputy Doofus," Frank muttered to Terry.

"Watch it," Wendy warned them.

Quinn felt his face burning up.

Maria crouched down, craning her neck to look inside the car. "Guys," she said, "I think I see something." She shimmied forward, clay up to her ankles.

"Be careful," Quinn told her. "We don't know if—"

The car's radio blared static so loud Quinn had to cover his ears. Hector and Wendy jumped, moving towards their bikes. Maria scrambled backwards, slipping and falling with a loud *squish* as Rick "Madman" Wade's voice came from the ruined Delorean's speakers, warped and going in and out of tune.

"And now a special request from one of our listeners. They write: Dear Madman, this summer has been a lonely one. Sometimes the music is the only thing that makes it better. Keep those records spinning. Well, this one's for you, Lonely, wherever you are. Hope your blues hit the skids real soon."

Quinn felt his chest tighten as "Glow Worm" played from the smashed car.

"*When the night falls silently,*
The night falls silently on forests dreaming..."

"This can't be real," Hector said. "I'm dreaming, right?"

"You're not," Wendy told him. "I can pinch you if you want."

Maria picked herself up out of the muck. Terry and Frank were already hauling butt down the path, screaming.

"Guys! Wait up!"

She shot the Crypt Crew the dirtiest look she could before following after them. "See you at home, Hector," she spat over one shoulder.

Hector cringed, stepping behind Wendy.

Midnight Crooners sang from the DeLorean's speakers, their voices melding with the chirps of birds and squirrels in the trees. The car fell dead, the music stopping to let an uneasy silence fall over the Crew.

"Guys," Hector said. "We're not cursed, right?"

"Did you offend a witch and not tell us?" Wendy asked.

"No. I mean, I don't think so. Unless Mrs. Ruane is a secret witch. I accidentally trampled her garden a few weeks back."

A twig snapped loudly behind them. Quinn scanned the darkening forest, trying to see through the thick shadows around clustered tree trunks.

"Time to vamos," Hector said. "Now!"

They pedaled as fast as they could away from the car, "Glow worm" fading into the woods. Quinn looked over his shoulder. He couldn't shake the feeling that someone had been watching them.

Or some*thing*.

The Thing Behind the Falls

Wendy's father came out to greet them as the Crypt Crew raced into the dirt lot of the ranger station.

"Kids? What are you doing here?"

When Wendy told him about the car, he raced into the station. The Crew followed him in.

"Henry, come in," he said into the radio.

"I'm here, Dale." Quinn felt a bit better when he heard his brother's voice.

"I got the kids here," Mr. Francis said. "Something happened to Martin." He lowered his voice, trying to cover the receiver with a hand. "Looks like the Snatcher."

Calmly, though Quinn could hear the strain in Henry's voice, he told Mr. Francis to wait while he got a tow truck.

"Alright," Mr. Francis said, "I'm going to meet Henry at the scene. I want you kids to lock the door behind me. Wendy, if you see anything, and I mean anything that doesn't look right, call on the radio, there."

"I will, Dad. Be careful."

Hector locked the door as Mr. Francis left.

"Okay," he said, "You guys heard that thing in the woods too, right? I wasn't just imagining it?"

"No," Quinn said. "I heard it."

"I felt it," Wendy said. "Like prickles on my neck."

"So it could still be out there." Hector walked over to the nearest window, standing on tiptoes. "This is crazy. We should have told your dad."

"Yeah, but what? That we heard a twig snap? Felt some kind of strange eyes on us?"

Hector let out a frustrated huff. "Is it any weirder than finding a car crushed like a tin can, covered in clay, with the radio coming to life like Frankenstein?"

Quinn couldn't argue with that. He pictured his brother standing there with Mr. Francis, the both of them scratching their heads at the bizarre scene. He walked to the window that faced the Falls, their town's namesake and point of pride. The afternoon sun sparkled off the water as it cascaded off the mountain, sending a rainbow dancing across the treetops. A walking path wound up behind the falls and into caves that cut into the rock like a beehive. Quinn had spent his whole life exploring those caves. Every time he did, he felt like he was in some other world, pretending that when he emerged from behind the waterfall he'd be on another planet, or in some lost, prehistoric jungle where dinosaurs still roamed. To him, the Falls had always been a place of magic, the rushing water acting like some sort of portal into the imagination, a curtain into another realm.

Now the caves in all their mist and shadow made him uneasy. Yet more places for this clay-slinging Snatcher to hide out.

Quinn felt an arm on his shoulder.

"Hello? Earth to Quinn."

Quinn was about to answer when something moved behind the Falls. He saw it for a brief moment before it disappeared into the cave.

No, he thought.

Impossible.

Inside one of the caves, a large piece of rock had moved. It wavered at first, shimmering like something under water and then shambled. It was *alive*!

A long limb reached out. Behind it, for a split second, Quinn could make out a second figure, mostly hidden in shadow. It lurched up behind the moving rock, seeming to usher it along, until both were hidden behind the waterfall.

He staggered away from the window.

"What is it?" Wendy asked.

"I—" he stopped himself, pressing his face closer to the glass, studying the Falls. "I saw it."

"It?" Hector sidled up beside him. "What is it?"

"I...I don't know. Something strange." He pointed to the cave behind the waterfall. "It just went in there."

"Okay," Hector said, turning to Wendy. "Your dad keep any weapons here?"

She shook her head. "None for you."

"Well *excuse* me for trying to protect us."

"The only weapon you're good with is your Atari controller," Wendy said.

"Hector, take it easy," Quinn said. He was still frozen in place.

"It could be him," Wendy said. "I'm calling it in."

Henry and Mr. Francis spent the next hour searching the Falls, returning to the ranger station with mud-soaked ponchos.

"Well?" Hector pressed.

"Nothing," Henry said. He took off his hat and shook water from the brim. "You sure about what you saw, Quinn? I mean, can you describe it again?"

"It looked like a person," Quinn said.

"Tall?"

"Yes," he said. "The shadow thing, at least."

"And the..." Henry pinched the bridge of his nose, clearly frustrated, "the other thing. The rock. Could it have been a kid?"

Quinn shook his head. "I don't think so. Henry, it didn't look like a human. Its arms were long, thin as noodles, and the skin was red and brown like, like—"

"Clay." Henry finished for him.

"Yes," Quinn said. He felt his cheeks redden when he saw the way Mr. Francis and Henry were both looking at him. "But honest, it was, it was—"

"Enough," Henry said. "Quinn, please." He rubbed at the dark bags under his eyes. "You kids have seen too many weird things these past few days. It's getting to you. It's getting to all of us."

"Too many ghoul and goblin stories," Mr. Francis said. "And you wonder why I don't keep any of that trash in the house. I don't know what your mother was thinking, allowing you to read and watch all that stuff. Scaring yourself half to death is fun these days? I don't get it."

"Dad, that's not true. If Quinn says he saw it, then that's what he saw."

"Maybe the monsters are real this time," Hector said. "How else do you explain what happened to Martin's car?"

Mr. Francis could only shrug at that.

"Maybe," Henry said, his voice froggy from lack of sleep.

"I'm not lying," Quinn said, "and my mind isn't playing tricks on me."

Henry nodded slowly. "Okay, pal. I know you're not lying." He let out a long, tired sigh. "We checked the caves, top to bottom. No trace of anyone squatting in there. No footprints. No nothing. Whatever you saw, it didn't hang around very long."

"Maybe it went into the tunnels," Hector said.

"Those tunnels don't go anywhere, son," Mr. Francis said. "They just circle around, or stop at dead ends. Plus, you can barely squeeze into 'em. Raccoons might use them, that's about it."

A car horn honked outside. Henry waved to Mr. Arpin in his tow truck.

"Alright," he said. "I'm going to head down with Jacques and bring Martin's car to the station. I'll drop everyone off at home first."

"But we're supposed to help Mr. Malman at the shop," Hector said.

"He'll be fine," Henry said, motioning for them to follow.

"Come on, guys." Wendy said, walking to the door. "We can work on the story at your house, Q."

Mr. Francis held her back. "I want you here. You can see your friends tomorrow. Taking a break from those horror stories may be just what you need."

Wendy crossed her arms, staring daggers at her father.

"We'll see you tomorrow," Quinn said to her, trying to sound cheerful. "And we'll work on *The Sound in the Walls* at Malman's, first thing."

"Great," Mr. Francis said softly under his breath. "More stories. More *art*."

Wendy shoved past him, taking a seat on the worn couch by his desk, resting her chin on her fists.

"What?" Mr. Francis said, flustered. "What did I say?"

"That's the problem, Dad. You don't even hear it."

"*Martin?*"

Mr. Malman fell back tiredly onto the stool behind the counter.

"He was one of my Ethan's best friends. I watched him grow into a fine young man. Randall, too." He shook his head. "And your brother, and Brent Foster. The four of them were inseparable, you know. Like you two and Wendy." He leaned forward. "Cherish your time together, boys. That's all I can say. These summers…summers of youth…they never last. Not as long as we hope they will."

Hector raised his eyebrows at Quinn. "Wow, Mr. Malman. That's a little dark."

Mr. Malman smiled, though Quinn could see it was forced. "Maybe a bit," the old man admitted. "I just…I worry about you kids. The world is a dangerous place. And it only seems to get worse. Even in a place like Stark Falls, you can never be sure."

"Well no one's dead yet," Hector said matter-of-factly. "Just missing."

Mr. Malman gave a weak nod, as if he were half listening.

"At least something's happening in this town," Hector went on. "Quinn even saw something. Well he *says* he saw something, right Quinn?"

Mr. Malman sat up straighter, the lines of his face creasing.

"It…" Quinn began, but stopped himself. "It was nothing. Really, Mr. Malman."

"Oh, come on!" Hector said, "you told me—"

Under the counter, Quinn slammed his foot on top of Hector's shoe. He let out a pained grunt.

"Honest," Quinn said. "It was just a trick of the light or something. I don't know why *someone* would even bother mentioning it."

Malman was standing, now, stooped over the counter.

"But if you did see...something amiss, you would tell your brother, yes?"

"Of course." Quinn studied Malman's face and saw penetrating fire in the old man's eyes.

He's worried, Quinn figured.

And Hector certainly wasn't helping matters, talking about monsters in caves.

Malman relaxed a bit, then. "You kids are my family, you know. My children," he chuckled, "at least on weekends and school vacations. I don't want anything happening to you. So bear with me, and heed some advice from an old man, will you? Don't go wandering around the Falls. Or Stark River. They're not safe in the best of times, and especially not with some maniac on the loose. If something were to happen to either of you, or to Wendy..." he let the matter settle there.

"We won't," Quinn said. As the words left his lips, he knew they weren't true. He didn't tell him about the thing in the Falls because he didn't think the old man needed anything more to worry about. Didn't he have enough already? Didn't everyone?

Malman nodded. "Good."

The front door jangled as Mr. Arpin entered. The large man was dressed in his oil-splattered work coveralls and looked like he hadn't slept all night. Normally, he gave a wide, white-toothed smile, jovial and always with a quick, gut splitting joke. Especially with the Crypt Crew. But that afternoon, Quinn thought he looked like a man who'd just seen a ghost.

Or worse.

"Afternoon, Jacques," Mr. Malman said.

"Afternoon, Jonas."

"You alright? Look like you could use a good sit down. Quinn, why don't you fetch Mr. Arpin here a soda."

"Thanks, gents." Mr. Arpin took a seat at the counter. He looked over to Quinn and Hector.

"Nasty business, last night. You boys alright?"

"We're okay," Quinn answered.

"Hardly," Hector replied, thumbing through an issue of *Famous Monsters*.

"Well, I can't say I blame you." He nodded in thanks as Quinn slid a cold glass of root beer along the counter.

"Been strange, these past few days." His eyes seemed to glaze, and he took a long sip of his soda. The boys leaned against the counter, watching.

Quinn had always thought of Mr. Arpin as the coolest guy in town. He carried himself with ease, the only real jazz musician within a hundred miles, probably. He worked all over town, fixing this and that, doing odd jobs for everyone. There wasn't a gizmo or gadget he couldn't figure out. He was a keen hunter, too, and carried himself like he'd been around the world twice over.

Seeing him in that state didn't help Quinn's growing unease.

"Things haven't been right, boys. I think anyone can tell you that."

"How do you mean?" Hector asked. Quinn could hear the excitement, or was it fear, in his friend's voice?

"No," Mr. Arpin said, and let out a laugh. "You'll think I'm going crazy. Jonas will, too."

"I'd never think that, and you know it," Mr. Malman said. "So what's the story?"

Mr. Arpin set his glass down and looked at the magazine in Hector's hands.

"You wanna know something? I used to read those horror rags all the time. Couldn't get enough of 'em." He shook himself. "Now? Don't know how you boys read that stuff, with all this strangeness happening 'round town. Gives me the heebie jeebies."

"What happened, Jacques?" Mr. Malman asked.

"Nothing happened. Well, nothing really. Just a feeling I've had since last night. Feeling like something's watching me. Around midnight I was finishing up locking Martin's car in the town garage when something, and I *swear* it was something, banged on the big loading bay door. But I looked outside and couldn't see more than a nose in front of me. So I go about my night like always. Fixing a few chainsaws for the Lumber Yard, getting Mr. Todd's tractor in shape. Then outside by the bins, I hear this...this..."

"What?" Quinn asked.

"Can't say for sure. But I tell you this, it wasn't some animal. Heck, I doubt it was a person. Sounded like something slimy, something big workin' its way through a big, sloshy pool of muck. I tell you right now, something was out there with me. Ploppin' and shufflin'. Like some kinda slug slitherin' itself along." He drained the glass of soda, collecting himself. "I finished up around six this morning. Took every ounce of courage I had to go out there and see what was what. And you know what I found? A big mound of clay. Clay! Same stuff that covered Martin's car like some kinda cocoon. How's that for a story, huh?" He paused. "Funny thing, too. I turn around, and guess who's standing there? Rabbi Shwartz, of all people. Scared me half to death in that big black coat, looking like some kind of gravedigger." He winced. "Sorry, Jonas. I asked him what brought him round so early. He looked at me funny, you know how he does, and says he's been 'looking out for something'. Something like this? I pointed to the clay. He stares at the stuff for a long time, then turns and walks off. Not even a goodbye or good morning. What do you think, kids? Time for old Mr. Arpin to get taken away by men in white coats and sent to the happy hospital?"

"Doesn't sound like nothing to me," Hector said quietly. "Sounds like we're about to be swallowed up by *The Blob*."

"Come on, now," Mr. Malman said. "I think you're scaring the boys."

"Heh!" Mr. Arpin laughed, gesturing to the horror magazines. "You kiddin'? These kids have nerves of steel. More than me and you, I can tell you that. No, I'm the one who's scared, is all. Just nice to be out in the sunlight. This town seems to fall apart when the sun goes down." He looked at Quinn. "Your brother hot on this perp's trail?"

"Yes, sir."

Mr. Arpin leaned forward and tousled Quinn's hair. "Henry's a good boy. He'll find 'em. And when he does, I'll feel a whole lot better about workin' nights."

"Agreed," Mr. Malman said. "Everyone's on edge, Jacques. The sooner Henry catches this Snatcher of ours, the sooner everyone will feel safe."

The bell jangled as Mrs. Ruane entered, followed by a pack of ladies from the Garden Club.

"Coffee, Jonas." She barked.

"At once, your highness." Mr. Malman turned and gave the boys a sly wink.

Mrs. Ruane tilted her head to the side, hoisting up her ear trumpet. "What was that?"

"I said one cup coming up!"

Mrs. Ruane scowled, fixing her attention on Mr. Arpin.

"You found the Ward boy's car?"

"No, but these gents did," he said, nodding to the boys. "And how'd you hear about that?"

"Never you mind," she snapped. She whirled on Quinn. "You tell that Deputy brother of yours that I want whoever this is caught. Caught this instant! We have our annual Garden Showcase next month, and I will not tolerate some *brute* in our midst!" The women behind her nodded in agreement.

"Hey, now," Mr. Arpin said, "He's doing the best he can. Give him some time."

"Time?" Mrs. Ruane snapped. "Time is what we do not have, Jacques Arpin. This is a nice town. A peaceful town. And this Snowshoe *what's-his-name* is besmirching its good name, and our reputation! The whole county will be here, and I refuse to have those old bats from the Elmwood Garden Society looking down their noses at us!"

"One coffee, nice and hot," Mr. Malman said, cutting her off.

Everyone was grateful for the silence that followed as she gulped it down.

Malman shuffled himself around the counter, pausing by the stockroom door.

"Before you go, I have something for the two of you. Three, if you'll give Wendy hers."

Hector perked up.

"Saw them in the sportsman's catalogue and thought of you right away." He disappeared into the stockroom, returning moments later with three long cardboard boxes. The sides read **OLD WEST COMPLETE BOW AND ARROW SET**. Quinn and Hector looked at one another, practically bursting at the seams.

"Really? For us?"

"Well," Malman said, shrugging with the boxes in hand, "I got more for the store, of course. I'm sure the other kids will want to get their hands on these. But I wanted you three to be my very first customers."

"Wow!" Mr. Arpin exclaimed from the soda counter. "I thought toy pop guns were the thing, but you know, I always sided with the Indians, myself. My old man said we had some Pequot in us."

"These must've cost a fortune," Hector said, taking one of the boxes and holding it to his chest. "I mean, I'll have to work double shifts just to pay it back!"

"No charge," Mr. Malman said. "With all that's been going on, I thought you three could use some distraction." He winked. "Maybe give you some protection, as well. You spend all your money on the arcade, anyhow."

Hector took the box, suddenly struggling for words, "Thanks, Mr. Malman!"

"You're very welcome, Mr. Delgado. But I'd hide that from your mother. I don't think the town doctor will take kindly to her boy shooting arrows in the backyard."

"Wonderful," Mrs. Ruane said. "Now you're arming the children, Jonas?"

Mr. Malman sighed. "Toys, Edna. Just some toys."

The old woman let out a loud grunt of searing disapproval. "And I see you haven't sold any of our dolls. I guess no one in this town wants the bridge repaired, eh? Pitiful. Come on, ladies." She ushered her followers out the door like a grouchy shepherd.

Before the door closed behind them, she poked her head back inside. "And Jacques, someone trampled my garden last night. Clay everywhere! I expect to have it cleaned by this afternoon!"

The boys and the men shared a long, concerned look at that.

"It's disgusting!" Mrs. Ruane said. "And it smells like a sewer. My poor tulips! Hmpf!" The bell jingled noisily as she left.

"Can't say I'm sorry to see them leave," Mr. Malman said quietly.

"More clay," Mr. Arpin said. "Like it's, I dunno, invading the place."

Quinn paused at that, thinking of *Invaders from Mars*. Was it coming from space? Creeping its way across the whole town? That would explain the noises. And the smell. He shook the thought from his head.

"Quinn, we're stashing these at your place," Hector said, pulling him from his troubling thoughts.

Quinn took one of the boxes from Mr. Malman, cradling it under his arm.

"Sure," he said. "No problem." *Along with your fireworks, cap guns, potato-shooters, boomerangs, and throwing stars.* "And thank you, Mr. Malman. For everything."

"You're very welcome. Now I think it's time you two get going. I'll be fine on my own today, so long as Jacques doesn't decide to drink up all my ice cream soda."

"Hey," Mr. Arpin said, "I just might take you up on that." He flashed a grin. "You boys ride safe, and keep an eye out for them cavalry men. Us braves gotta watch out for each other." He mimed pulling back the string of a bow, then spun round on his stool.

Quinn and Hector raced against the coming dusk, thundering down empty streets, the wheels of their bikes crunching over twigs and splashing through puddles where hoses lay running in flower beds and against fences near the curb, sprinkling their shins with icy bursts of water in the molasses-thick New Hampshire heat.

To Quinn, it felt as if they were the last kids on the whole planet, left to roam the neighborhood while the adults were stuck at the ironworks or down in the textile mill, or bunkered up in their homes with locked doors and their eyes glued to the news, ever vigilant in case the Snowshoe Snatcher decided to take a third victim. He kept one arm snugly around his new bow and arrow set, feeling a bit more confident, even if it was just a toy. At the moment, it was all he had.

As they neared Quinn's driveway, a wood-paneled station wagon came to a halt, blocking their path. Hampton Harwich exited the car, his eyes wild.

"Boys! I've been looking all over for you!" he cried.

"Us?" Hector asked, "why?"

"For my next story!" he looked to the sky, extending his arms like he was reading off the ticker-tape in Times Square. "The disappearance of Martin Ward! You were the ones who found his car, yes?"

Quinn felt uneasy beneath the newspaper man's eager gaze.

"Well, yeah, but we really don't—"

"Not another word," Harwich said. "Meet me at the office as soon as you can. I'd love an interview with some locals." He clapped. "Oh, this is just so exciting, isn't it boys? When I write this up, it'll be award winning. Pulitzer stuff! Move over, Truman Capote!"

Without a glance at the boys, he threw himself back into the car, peeling towards town before Quinn could even respond.

A Midnight Adventure

"Watch this!" Hector drew back the bow, sweat beading his brow as he aimed the arrow. He took a deep breath, arms trembling from the strain, and let it fly with a loud *twang* of the string. The arrow sailed almost too fast for Quinn to follow before it thunked into its target, the feathered end vibrating from the force. Hector took a step back and gave Quinn an exaggerated bow.

"And I wasn't even trying on that one!"

Quinn looked to the wooden targets set up in his backyard. Each of them were life size cutouts of their favorite characters. They'd spent the last summer building them, mostly for Hector, who wanted a place for slingshot target practice far from the prying eyes of his mother.

Quinn walked up to the life-sized Dracula, which Wendy had painted, and pried the arrow from between the vampires' red, menacing eyes.

He wished she were with them, but her dad wanted her safe at home.

"Not trying, huh? Sure looked like you were sweating a lot there, hot shot."

"Hey, I'm a hefty kid. Mom says it's a healthy weight. Can't help it if I sweat a bit."

Quinn drew an arrow from the plastic quiver and went about

nocking his own bow, drawing it up until the string was nearly pressed against his right eye. He aimed next to Dracula, where Jason Vorhees lurked, ready to pounce just beyond the Katz' backyard fence.

He let loose, watching the arrow sail just over the killer's head and thud into the fence.

"Nice one, sharpshooter," Hector said, giving him a walloping smack on the back.

"Can't concentrate, is all."

Hector fiddled with the string on his bow, then gestured to the targets. Quinn looked from Dracula to Jason.

"What?" Quinn asked.

"It's nothing," Hector said. "I mean, it's not nothing, but it's dumb, I guess."

"Out with it," Quinn urged.

"It's just I never really thought monsters were real. Not until today. Did you?"

Quinn didn't know how to answer that, so he nodded slowly.

"I mean, we're always reading about them, watching them at the drive in. Coming up with our own. But that was all for fun. Being scared is *fun*. But not like this. It's so real, now. The Snatcher really is out there, somewhere. Mr. Arpin heard something. So did Clark. How many others?"

"Henry will catch him."

Hector lowered his bow. "Him?"

"The Snatcher. Or whatever it is they decide to call him."

Hector folded his arms. "You still think it's a *him*?"

Quinn shrugged. "What am I supposed to think it is?"

Hector pointed to the targets again.

"What?" He looked over his shoulder, where the wooden Dracula still had an arrow poking through his head. "Think it's a vampire?"

"I sure as heck don't think it's some random guy. We're dealing with a monster, here. I can't be the only one who sees it." He laughed nervously. "You know, my Abuela always told me that we've had many brujos and brujas in our family. Witches. Sorcerers. The stories she has… old legends about one of my great, great grandmothers dealing with ghosts or demons. I always thought she was kidding. But who knows? All those stories of monsters, they have to come from somewhere, right?

Like fairy tales. There's always some smidge of truth." He shrugged. "Maria says she's crazy. But Maria says that about everyone."

Quinn nodded, uneasy. He felt the same way. Lately, the idea of a monster on the loose didn't seem as fun as it used to. Now that it was real, or seemed to be, the stakes felt very, very high.

"And what about Mr. Arpin's story? Rabbi Shwartz didn't seem so surprised when he saw the clay. And what's this 'looking out for the town' stuff? It doesn't sound right."

"No, it doesn't," Quinn agreed, remembering the red dust on the rabbi's clothes. The man was almost a recluse, the way he stayed in that tiny synagogue at the edge of town. If someone was really 'looking out' for everyone, Quinn doubted it was the rabbi.

"Maybe he's controlling the Snatcher. Like how Doctor Frankenstein controls the monster. Or Dracula controls Renfield."

Now that was a scary thought.

Quinn had been scared of Rabbi Shwartz ever since he could remember. When his father died and his family sat shiva, he'd been too terrified to go into the family room, where the rabbi stayed and prayed with Henry and the neighbors. The man's cold eyes gave him the chills.

"And we're the only ones who know about it," he said.

"You have to make your brother believe," Hector said. "If we can't convince him, what can we do? The other kids know something's not right, either. Terry and Frank, Abbie and Clark. Even Maria's acting jittery. And that's saying something."

As Quinn struggled to come up with an answer, he heard Henry's car pull into the driveway. They stored their bows and arrows alongside the shed as Henry entered the backyard.

"Good to see you fellas are keeping busy," he said, nodding to the monster targets. "Your mom called me at the station, Hector. Wants me to give you a lift home. You ready? Go on and throw your bike in the back."

Hector looked back to Quinn, his eyes serious as he mouthed "*talk to him*".

"I will," Quinn said quietly.

Hector followed Henry through the yard and out to the car. The sun was setting as the car backed down the drive, and as Quinn stood alone in the grass, he felt the all-too-familiar sensation of eyes, hidden and hungry, watching him from some shadowed corner. Fighting the chill that raced through his veins, he walked quickly to the back door, locking it before sprinting to his room.

Quinn spent the better part of the night touching up his models. He had quite a collection from Malman's: A Creature from the Black Lagoon, Godzilla (which was finally done), a glow in the dark Frankenstein, and King Kong. But even as he carefully dabbed paint on the plastic figures, he found it hard to keep his concentration. Instead, he focused on what he'd seen at the Falls, that brief glimpse of a shuffling form vanishing into the caves and the shadowy figure moving beside it. He knew it wasn't a trick of the eye. And he was fairly sure he wasn't losing it.

A knock at the door pulled him from his frustrated daydream.

"Come in," he said, putting the caps back on his paints as Henry walked in.

Henry looked far older than his twenty-one years. His normally square shoulders we slumped, and he sat down heavily on the foot of Quinn's bed. He held a sheaf of papers in a worn folder, and as he sat, dozens of them slid out onto the bed.

Quinn sat next to him, his feet dangling off the bed while Henry's reached the floor.

Quinn glanced down at the spilled pile of letters. On each one was written "**Stark Falls Sheriff's Office**" in bold letters.

"Messages left at the station," Henry said tiredly. "Mabel's been getting calls from sunup to sundown over there."

Quinn saw one of the letters read "WHY ISN'T THE DEPUTY DOING MORE? THIS TOWN DESERVES BETTER!"

Another, also in all capital letters, read "WE NEED KATZ OUT AND TOOHEY BACK IN. FOLKS ARE SCARED TO LEAVE THEIR HOMES AT NIGHT!"

Still another: "IF KATZ CAN'T COPE, GET RID OF HIM!"

"Oh," Henry said, and tossed the latest issue of the Minuteman on the bed. The headline read: **Ineffective Deputy Failing at His Job?**

Clearly, Hampton Harwich, that intrepid journalist, was feeling particularly vindictive.

"Jeeze," Quinn said, unable to come up with anything brighter. "Are you okay?"

Henry was silent for a while. Quinn watched as he swallowed, his lips trembling slightly.

"No. Not really," he admitted. "Quinn, I feel like I'm in way over my head, here. Can't make heads or tails of it." He sighed, shoulders heaving. "I never expected to wind up in a situation like this, you know?"

"I know," Quinn said.

"The whole town looks to me to protect them. But what am I protecting them from?" He let out a frustrated sigh. "Randall and Martin. They can't be gone. Not really. I know those guys. I grew up with them. They couldn't just *disappear*. They wouldn't allow it. Never. And now the station's getting calls calling for me to resign. Harwich started a whole column just to trash my reputation." He laughed bitterly. "And to think, folks called me a hero not too long ago."

"Are you sleeping okay?"

"No," Henry said. "The dreams are back. Worse than before."

Quinn was about to put his hand on Henry's shoulder when his brother turned and looked him in the eye.

"I...I'll tell you about them."

Quinn felt his heart lurch in his chest. He wasn't sure if he wanted to hear about Henry's nightmares. He wasn't sure if he was ready. But the look in Henry's eyes told him that he needed someone to hear.

Quinn needed to be there for his brother.

"Only if you want to," he said.

Henry closed his eyes. "I think I have to, pal. It's only right you should know. Randall and Martin and Brent...they were the only ones I could ever talk with. The only ones who understand. But you're my brother. You've helped me, and in the end, you're all I've got." He gestured to the letters. "And if I don't get my head right and solve this case soon, you'll be the only person in town who'll even speak to me."

Henry was shaking.

"You can tell me."

"We were spending the last week of summer together," he started, his voice very faint. "It was really a sendoff for Ethan. He got accepted to Dartmouth. Only one of us who got into college."

Quinn winced, hearing Ethan's name.

"We had Martin's boat. We'd saved for it for a year. We drove up to the Canadian line and took the Stark River all the way down, rapids and all. It was a good trip. Good weather, and the rapids were pretty rough. We were just past Pike's Landing when we heard the shouts." He took Quinn's hand in his own, squeezing. "We found two canoes, big ones that fit about six people each. One was capsized. The other was stuck in a whirlpool in the middle of a ring of sharp rocks. They were kids. Nature Scouts. Martin and I rowed as hard as we could, pulling over to the side. Brent jumped off and used a rope to moor us. Some of the kids were clutching onto the rocks. Others to the boat. The ones in the whirlpool were screaming. Crying for their parents. A lot of them were bleeding. I'm telling you, those rocks were sharp as razors. One kid wasn't moving at all. His life vest saved him. Water just kept him pinned, his shoulder bleeding out. We knew we had to jump in there. They couldn't resist the current that much longer. I hauled out a few, then Martin, then Randall. But the kids holding on to the other canoe were still stuck, and the driftwood holding the boat in place was starting to give way. Ethan told us that if we didn't get them before it snapped, they'd be sucked under. So he jumped. Dove right in. I swear he swam against that current like a salmon. He brought seven kids back. He was braver than all of us. I was so scared I could barely see, let alone think straight. He kept his cool. He kept them alive."

Henry's voice was cracking the more he spoke, and Quinn could feel his pulse hammering as he squeezed harder onto his hand.

"I could see how tired he was," he continued. "Martin and I reached out for him when Brent lost control of the rope. Our boat rushed forward and slammed into the rocks." He showed Quinn the scars. "I was bleeding a lot, but I didn't care. Ethan was still in there. Martin tried to jump out, but the rapids whipped our boat around, and while he was trying to get into the water, we were smashed against the rocks again and his leg was shattered."

Quinn could feel the tears forming in his eyes. He never knew that. Martin had carried that wound silently, all this time.

"We couldn't get to him in time. I would have kept going. I would have given up this arm to save him, but it was too late. Ethan went under, and that's the last I saw."

Henry began to sob into his hands. Quinn wrapped an arm around his shoulder.

"It's okay," he said. "It's okay, Henry."

"They didn't find him until the next day. He was…Oh, Quinn! I see him every time I close my eyes. When we got home, I tried telling Mr. Malman…tried to tell him what Ethan did for us. For all of those kids. He just stared at me. Shut the door in my face. A few months later, someone vandalized Ethan's grave. The headstone was cracked, and it looked like someone had tried digging up the coffin. I don't know if he ever told you that. It was my first case as a Deputy. I tried my best, but came up empty handed. Malman never forgave me for that. I don't think he ever will." He sighed. "I'm glad he likes you. But every day I think about what Ethan did for us. For *them*. Every day I regret that I didn't do more. I should have been with him. Should have…should have…" Henry turned and drew Quinn into a tight embrace. Quinn let himself cry, feeling Henry's hot tears on the side of his face. Henry's whole body heaved as he let himself go, allowed himself to let go, for the first time in a long time.

"When I took this job, I swore I'd be like Ethan. I'd never pick up a gun, never hurt a living soul. I wanted to help people. Protect them." He pulled himself away, wiping his eyes. "And what happens? I lost two of my best friends. Just like I lost Ethan. Now the whole town looks to me. I have no answers for them. Not one. I'm scared, Q. And alone."

"You're not alone," Quinn told him.

Henry smiled sadly. "I know I have you, pal. But when I'm out in that car, wearing that badge, it sure feels like I'm on my own."

"I'm glad you told me," Quinn said. "I know it was hard, but I'm glad you did it. You don't have to be afraid. And I'll always be here."

"I know, pal. I know."

Quinn was about to ask him about the caves, about the thing that he saw. But at that moment, he didn't think Henry would take it well. He hadn't seen what Quinn had seen.

Hector's words echoed in his mind.

You have to make your brother believe.

"I have to get some shuteye," Henry said, rising. "Tomorrow I'll have to call this in to the State Police. Randall's been gone three days. That makes him an official missing person. Maybe they'll send out some folks to help. I could use the help."

"I'll have the coffee ready," Quinn said.

Henry smiled, leaned forward to ruffle Quinn's hair.

"Thanks." His smile suddenly faded, and he studied Quinn's face. "Promise me you'll keep an eye out. Be vigilant. Isn't that what Dad always used to say?"

Quinn nodded. Their father had always told them, 'be alert, be vigilant, be aware of your surroundings'. It seemed to be his mantra. Quinn never really took it to heart. Hearing it from Henry's mouth shook him.

"I will."

"Good. Night, Q."

Quinn waited on his bed, listening to Henry's footsteps recede down the hallway. When he heard his bedroom door shut, he leapt up and picked up the phone, dialing as fast as he could.

If there was a monster out there, maybe there was something they could do. The Crypt Crew would join the case. For Henry.

He lifted the receiver, listening until Hector picked up.

"Hey," he said, covering the mouthpiece in case Henry was still awake. "I want you to meet me at the mill."

"What, tonight?" Hector hissed. "Are you watching *Nightmare Theater*? They're showing *The Blob*! Can you believe it? How weird is that?"

"Midnight," Quinn said. "And I want you to call Wendy, too. We're checking out the Falls."

"Quinn, I don't think—"

"Henry needs us," Quinn said urgently. "The town needs us."

"Us? What can we do?"

"We know about monsters," Quinn told him. "More than anyone. And if you're right about this, we might be the only ones with the knowledge to stop it."

Hector was silent for a moment. "My mom's working late," he said. "I can meet up no problem. But Quinn?"

"Yeah?"

"You'd better bring my supplies."

Quinn knew "supplies" meant the stash of dangerous toys and weapons he kept in the Katz's shed.

"Which ones?"

"Well," Hector said, "we're hunting a monster, right? So, all of them."

Quinn usually liked Castelot's Textile mill at night. Without the hum of the machinery and the billowing smokestacks sending white clouds into the air, the cars lining the parking lot and the shouts and laughter of the workers, it felt more like an abandoned factory.

The Crypt Crew always called it the Laboratory and would joke about how when the workers went home, a mad doctor took control, conducting his horrific experiments while the people of Stark Falls slept. Frank Castelot had told them about some strange things his father and the other workers had heard during long night shifts. There was a town legend about one of the Stark family members dying there, way back in the 1800's when they still owned it. Somehow, they either fell or dove into the textile processing machine, cut to ribbons. Rumor had it that the ghost of Ezra Stark still haunted the mill.

The Crew had written a story titled *The Ghost Mill* about it. It was the first one they'd ever sent out.

While Quinn waited in the silent parking lot, the Laboratory didn't seem so fun. Instead, the smokestacks and soot covered windows made it seem like building was alive, watching him, ready to tear itself out of the pavement and grasp him with brick and mortar fingers, suck him in and devour him with the huge manglers and compactors, crunching his bones with heavy iron teeth.

Get a grip, he told himself. *It's just a building*. He shifted the backpack he'd stuffed with Hector's boomerang, a throwing knife, bow, quiver of arrows, and three flashlights. *Save it for the* real *scary stuff*.

He jerked at the sound of tires on asphalt, and through the dim streetlights, saw Hector and Wendy pedaling fast into the parking lot. They both skidded to a stop, catching their breath.

"You guys sneak out okay?"

"Not a problem," Hector said. "Abuela's in bed by seven, Maria's doing her summer school work, and mom's making a house call across the river in Pike's Landing."

"Dad doesn't know I left," Wendy said. "He called my mom and told her what's been happening. Now she's demanding he send me packing to New York. He wasn't having it. I left before the real screaming started."

"Is he at the station?"

"It took a lot to convince him to stay home tonight," Wendy said. "He was going to bunk up there. He's been pacing back and forth through the living room all night, looking out the windows like something's about to break in."

"So he believes me?" Quinn asked hopefully.

"Well...*kinda*. He started thinking about the caves, how someone might try them as a hideout. All of a sudden he got real spooked."

"Yeah," Hector said. "Whole town is spooked. But he's not buying the 'shadow man' stuff that you were on about, Q."

"No one would," Quinn said. "And that's why we're going to check it out and prove it."

Wendy shifted on her bike. "Do you two really think this is smart? Going up there, just the three of us? I feel like we should have told somebody. You know, in case we don't come back." The last two words were whispers.

"Come *back*?" Hector laughed. "Of course we'll come back."

"Well, the Snatcher is still out there," Wendy said. She gestured to the mill. "Could be hiding in there watching us, for all we know."

"That's why I had Quinn bring the goods."

Quinn shrugged off his backpack. Wendy and Hector inspected the assortment. Wendy chose the boomerang, while Hector took the throwing stars, a box of matches, and an UNCLE SAM'S THUNDERBOLT firework rocket, which he aimed around like a spear, mimicking explosion sounds.

"Monster masher," he said, proudly cradling it in the crux of his arm. "Let's see our cave dweller stand up to this!"

"Don't get all macho on us," Wendy chided.

"I'm not getting macho," Hector retorted. "I already am macho. I can't help it. Tough hombres run in the family."

"I thought you were brujos and brujas," Quinn said with a smile.

"Them too. But brujos can be tough hombres, too." Quinn caught a glimpse of a fresh bruise Maria had given him. Hector quickly covered it up with his free hand.

Wendy let out an exasperated sigh. "How about we see what we're up against first, tough hombre?

Hector nodded, shimmying the rocket into the straps of his backpack. Wendy did the same with her boomerang, one edge peeking up over her shoulder. Quinn thought they looked like cavalry soldiers from some ancient battlefield, weapons strapped to their backs, bikes in place of war horses.

Armed and ready, the Crypt Crew set out from the mill's parking lot and up the empty roads. The streetlights were scarce as they left the center of town, pedaling up into the park's access road. Quinn slowed as they passed by the ditch where Martin's car had been. Under the moonlight he could make out the depressions in the ground where the DeLorean had overturned. Mud and clay still caked the ground, glistening like it was still fresh.

"You sure your dad is staying home tonight?" Hector asked as they approached the ranger station.

"I'm sure," Wendy said. "Anyway, he has to get up early to take the Scouts bird watching."

"Better safe than sorry," Quinn said, and held out a hand to stop them as he parked his bike behind a pine tree, craning his neck to peer at the station. No lights shone in the windows, and the small dirt lot was empty. Ahead, the sound of rushing water hissed through the trees.

They left their bikes on the side of the main hiking trail. The Falls loomed before them, cool mist tickling their faces. Hector took the lead, crouching, eyes wide and on full alert as they climbed the ever-rising trail until they were above the trees with the first set of caves before them.

Even in the dark, the Crypt Crew knew each of them. Generations of kids in Stark Falls had played in these caves, giving each one a name and a story to go along with it. Names like Grave Robber's Way, Dead Man's Rest, The Haunted Hallows, and Goblin Maze. Names that called to the imagination of countless kids, ringing of danger and adventure. Some were fabled hideouts of Revolutionary War spies, others the resting place of Native spirits, or secret bases for smugglers during Prohibition running booze down from Quebec. The most famous system, and one that the few tourists who came to Stark Falls always wanted to see, was Freedom's Reach, one leg of the Underground Railroad back in the 1800's.

They stopped at the first cave, Dead Man's Rest. It loomed behind the rushing water at the lowest part of the falls. Inside, a haphazard stairway of twisted and jagged rock led up, connecting to the other caves, the first of which was Grave Robber's Way, where Quinn had seen the rocks move and shimmer. Where the Snowshoe Snatcher could be hiding at that very moment, watching the trespassers enter his secret lair.

"Flashlights on," Wendy said.

The yellow beams sliced through the mist, illuminating the damp and glistening walls of Dead Man's Rest. Dark stone surrounded them, seeming to swallow them up as they took their first steps into the Falls.

INTO THE CAVES

"Here," Quinn said, extending the long piece of rope from his backpack. He looped one end around his waist and passed it down the line. "To make sure we don't get separated."

"Separated?" Wendy asked. "We could walk these caves blindfolded."

"I know."

"So why the rope?"

"Because—" Quinn caught himself, thinking of the way he saw the rocks move and melt like molding clay. "Just to be safe."

Wendy and Hector were silent, tightly fixing the length of rope to their waists, working it around while holding their flashlights in their mouths. When they were done Quinn thought they looked like mountain climbers, the ones he saw in *National Geographic* climbing the Himalayas.

"Lead on, Q," Hector said, hefting his backpack. He gestured to the rocky staircase. Quinn hoisted himself up, reassured by the slight pull of the rope at his waist. It was good to know his friends weren't far behind.

The rocky outcrop climbed up into the ceiling, where a small opening led to the next floor. It was just large enough for kids their size to wriggle through. *No way Henry and Mr. Francis made their way in here*, he thought, and as he pulled himself up, he was startled by the chirp and leathery flapping of a small bat. He cried out in surprise, then composed himself. If a bat could make him jump out of his socks, his monster hunting days would be short indeed.

"Trouble?" Wendy called, still at the base of the rocky steps.

"All clear!" Quinn called, his voice echoing off the walls. He climbed up into the second chamber, crawling forward on his elbows, the mineral scent of mud and stone filling his nostrils.

He aimed his flashlight in a circle, heart pounding as each shadowy corner of the cave was illuminated. With each turn of the flashlight, he feared the worst. The Snowshoe Snatcher smiling from the dark, lurking in that cramped, damp hovel. He shook the visions of ghosts and goblins from his head as Hector hoisted himself through the narrow opening, barely missing a sharp hanging stalagmite as he stood up. Wendy followed close behind.

A long piece of rock jutted from the cave mouth and through the waterfall. Kids called it the Diving Board. Quinn didn't think anyone had actually jumped from it, but Terry Pots and his buddies claimed they did two summers ago.

The rushing water looked like a shimmering curtain, the sound roaring in his ears. Quinn pushed through, jumping at the frigid blast. He could see the ranger station beyond, and the window he'd been standing in yesterday, looking in this very spot. The trees were dark blue beneath swaths of pale stars blotted out by the high peaks of the mountains.

He traced his steps to the exact spot he saw the movement. Behind him, two stalactites reached up from the floor. Small patches of grey and green lichen snaked over them like protruding veins, and when he shone the light, they seemed to glow like veins of some alien ore. He inched closer, waiting for them to move.

"These them?" Hector asked.

Quinn nodded, still staring.

"They don't look very alive," Wendy said.

"No," Quinn agreed. "But I swear it was right here. This was the spot." Just to be sure, he turned around and aimed his light at the ranger station, tracing the path.

Hector walked around the spires, poking and prodding the patches of moss with the butt of his flashlight. "They look like regular old rocks to me, Q."

Frustrated, Quinn waved his flashlight around the floor of the cave, looking for any trace of movement: a footprint, a scratch in the stone, disturbed dirt. Anything that marked that someone or something had been there recently.

"Let's try another cave," he said, turning to the entrance of the Goblin Maze.

"Wait!" Wendy hissed.

Quinn and Hector froze.

She took a few steps towards the wall, her light shining on a layer of slick-looking rock.

"This isn't supposed to be here." She scraped a thin layer of gooey clay from the wall with the edge of her boomerang.

The Crypt Crew studied the wall, watching globs of clay slowly drip down like melting wax.

"Is it the same stuff from Randall's place?" Hector asked.

"And Martin's car," Wendy said. "Someone put this here."

"Why?"

"It's covering something up," Wendy said.

"Alright," Hector said. He swung the UNCLE SAM'S THUNDERBOLT rocket from his backpack, whipped out a pack of matches, and aimed it at the wall like a bazooka.

"Ease up, there," Wendy said. "That stuff's not exactly dynamite, and the sound could cave this whole place in, Mr. Brujo." Taking the boomerang, she began slicing away at the clay. It came apart in tatters, surprisingly thin. In a few moments she'd uncovered an entrance to a tunnel the Crew had ever seen before. It was small, the walls and ceilings plastered with earth. It stank just like the stuff in Randall's house. Moldy and foul, like sewage.

Quinn took a few steps back, pulling Wendy and Hector along with him. He stared into the maw of the dark tunnel and realized that all his fears were coming true. There really *was* something in these caves. And it was hiding itself.

"What could have done this?" Hector asked, his voice shaky.

"It's new," Wendy mused. "But you'd have to have tools to do this. Big stuff. Dynamite and pickaxes. A tunnel boring machine, or—"

"Claws," Quinn said.

"Big ones," Hector muttered.

"Big enough to rip Randall Colburn's doors off their hinges," Quinn said. "Big enough to crush Martin Ward's car."

"Big enough to dig through stone," Wendy said.

Quinn nodded, skin prickling as a rush of cool air drifted from the clay-packed tunnel.

"Big enough to rip us to bite sized pieces," Hector said, cradling the firework. "So, who's first?"

The three friends stared into the darkness.

"This was my idea," Quinn said. "Guess that means me."

The hole was just large enough for Quinn to squeeze into, crawling on hands and knees through an inch thick layer of stinking clay. He wasn't normally claustrophobic, but he could feel his pulse quicken the further down he crept, the walls narrow and uneven. The tunnel sloped ever downward until he was sure they were underneath the Falls itself. He could no longer hear the rushing water. Only the faint whispers of wind in the dark and grunts of effort from Hector and Wendy as they crawled behind him.

Every now and then a glob of clay would smear the lens of his flashlight, casting him in darkness. In a panic, he'd clear it as best he could, always breathing a sigh of relief when the yellow light flickered back to life.

He was freezing cold, the clay soaking into his pants and his socks, sloshing around his shoes. He tried breathing through his mouth, the air thin, and the smell of mold so strong it was starting to make him dizzy.

"We should have brought a parakeet," Hector said, the cheeriness in his voice tinged with fear. "I'd have picked one up from the pet shop if I knew we were going down this far."

Quinn tried to laugh but couldn't find it in himself. With each inch he crawled into the dark, he realized that not even the bravest cave explorers would do something like this so unprepared. What if they got lost? Or couldn't turn back? The walls seemed to narrow, expanding and constricting like a pair of lungs.

Okay, he told himself. *Don't freak yourself out.*

"You can't back out now," he whispered, "Henry needs your help."

"Let's take a break," Wendy called from behind. "My legs are burning and I'm covered with this stuff."

Quinn felt the rope tighten around his waist as Hector and Wendy came to a halt. Just ahead, the tunnel forked, both openings high enough to stand in. He shimmied around until he could face them, grateful to see their faces in the light.

"So," Wendy breathed heavily, slicking the mud off her pant legs, "which way?"

Quinn wavered between the two tunnels. He had no idea how far down they'd already gone. He wiped away the muddy clay off his watch. It was almost one o'clock. Had they really been in these caves for an hour?

"I say left," Hector said.

"Any reason why?"

"Nope." He grinned in the flashlight beam under his chin. "One tunnel's as good as any, I guess."

They rested for a moment before continuing into the left tunnel. Quinn was glad to be able to stand upright. Still, he went slowly, training his light dead ahead. The mud and clay grew more slippery underfoot, and he had to hold onto the wall to steady himself.

Quinn stopped abruptly. Hector walked right into him, sending him sprawling onto the ground.

"Sorry!"

"Shh! Look!"

Hector paused, shining his light ahead.

"Do you see that?"

Wendy joined with her own light as Quinn, still on his knees, strained his eyes.

Quinn scooted closer. Very slowly, he prodded the object with his foot. It was a jacket, soaked and shredded.

"Look familiar?" Wendy asked.

Quinn shook his head. It was adult sized, though. Randall or Martin could have fit into it.

He continued on. Every few feet, there was another piece of clothing. A belt. A shoe. A sock. Quinn dreaded they would eventually stumble across the person who'd worn those clothes, somewhere in this dark, mud ridden abyss.

A glint of light bounced off the flashlight beam, golden and bright.

Quinn went to reach for it, but Hector stopped him. "Quinn, I don't like this." All the bravery was gone from his voice. "Let's go back, huh?"

"We've come this far," he said. "It might be something important."

"I know," he said, gesturing ahead. "But *listen*. Don't you hear that?"

A faint sound echoed in the dark. Something slowly moving through the mud.

Squish.

Squish.

Squish.

Quinn aimed his light back on the piece of gold. He could reach it. He knew he could.

"I'll grab it," he told them. "Then we run like crazy, okay?"

Hector and Wendy nodded, their faces streaked with mud.

"Just keep the rope tight," Wendy said. "In case we need to pull you out."

"I will," Quinn said. His stomach turned. He hoped it wouldn't come to that.

The wet *squishing* sounds grew louder as Quinn reached the object.

He sank his hand into the mud, touching something hard and square. He lifted it, straining under the pressure as he tried to dislodge it from the muck.

It was a gold-plated lighter in a silver case. Quinn used his shirt to clean off the caked mud.

"Guys, gimme some light?"

The air in the tunnel seemed to grow colder as the Crypt Crew studied the two letters engraved on the case.

M.W.

"Martin Ward," Quinn said.

"So this is where the Snatcher took him," Wendy said. "Those marks by his car. It dragged him awfully far."

"Okay," Hector said. "We got the evidence, now let's—"

His eyes grew wide and he let out a scream, pointing over Quinn's shoulder.

Quinn turned just in time to see something moving under the mud. Before he could step back, it gripped his ankle and yanked down hard.

The world went dark as he struggled against the immense strength. Mud filled his mouth and nostrils. He closed his eyes, fighting with everything he had to gain some footing, but he couldn't grip onto anything. The thing around his ankle tightened. Quinn fought for breath, trying to force his face up through the mud.

His mind exploded in panic. He'd end up like Randall and Martin. A victim of the Snatcher.

Please! Please, no! Further and further he was pulled into the dark, thick earth, buried alive, dragged down into his grave.

His lungs felt like they were about to burst. He opened his mouth on instinct and more mud poured in. It felt like he was being sucked into the pull of an undertow. He couldn't hold his breath any longer. Another couple of seconds and that'd be it. He could feel his heart race wildly, ready to burst in his chest, when suddenly he was pulled in the opposite direction with a painful yank. The rope around his waist tightened, pulling against the thing around his ankle.

It gave him just enough time to surface, and as his face broke through the layer of mud he sucked in a deep, ragged breath. His eyes were still caked in the stuff, but he could hear Wendy yelling "Pull! Pull!"

Quinn scrambled. He kicked savagely, with everything he had, until finally the thing in the mud released its grip. Exhausted, he turned around and began working his way back while Hector and Wendy reeled him in. By the time they hoisted him to safety, his arms and legs felt like jelly and his stomach churned. He vomited mud and clay.

Something let out a garbled screech in the dark.

Even though he could barely feel his own feet, Quinn raced behind Hector and Wendy, bolting back through the tunnel. They scrambled and pried their way through the narrow passageways until reaching the entrance to Grave Robber's Way. When they reached the cave and the sound of the Falls, Quinn felt a little better, but he'd lost his flashlight in the struggle, and when he turned back to the cave, all he could see was pitch dark. Whatever had grabbed him might be following just behind.

The Crew stumbled down the slick rocks. Hector tripped and pulled Quinn down with him, sliding onto the floor of the cave just at the edge of the Diving Board.

Even though Quinn was freezing cold, the mist from the water felt good, clearing some of the mud from his eyelids. His eyes adjusted to the moonlight. Quinn realized he still had Martin's lighter in his hand. He turned it around in the pale light, examining the initials.

"I can't believe it," he said. They'd done it. They'd found actual *proof* that something had taken Henry's friends. But as he looked at the lighter, he realized Martin and Randal were still down there, somewhere in all that darkness and muck.

Were they still alive? Being kept somewhere? And even if the Crypt Crew, Henry, and a whole search party went back down there, would they even find them?

"Guys, we should get moving," Wendy said. "That thing, whatever it was, it might not have to rest like we do."

Nerves on fire, every sound of the trail made Quinn flinch. The owls in the trees. The cry of a coyote in the woods. The great croak of a toad somewhere down river.

Even so, being out in the open was comforting. Even the buzz and bites of the nasty New Hampshire mosquitoes weren't quite as annoying.

"We'll stop by my house first," Quinn said. "Henry should still be asleep. We can use the hose out back."

"Good," Hector said. "If my mom finds me like this, she'll lock me in my room until high school. And if Maria sees me, she'll blab. She'd just love that."

They came to a wide bend in the trail, their bikes almost in sight when the orange light of a gas lantern swung from behind the trunk of a pine.

"Quick!" Wendy hissed, pulling the group behind a large boulder.

Quinn crawled up to the top, peeking his head over to get a look at the trail.

The figure holding the lantern was huge, his boots crunching loudly on the gravel. The lantern creaked as it swung side to side in his grasp. He paused, holding the light near his face. Quinn stifled a gasp.

Rabbi Shwartz scowled into the darkness, eyes searching the tree line.

Quinn pressed himself down onto the rock, perfectly still.

"What is it?" Hector whispered.

The rabbi swung to face the boulder.

"Who's there?" He demanded.

Quinn went to shimmy himself off the boulder to tell Hector to be quiet and lost his footing. The lighter flew from his hands, clattering down onto the trail.

"Show yourselves!" The rabbi thundered.

Quinn skidded to a stop where Hector and Wendy were hiding.

Wendy's face paled. "What's he doing here?"

"What do you think?" Hector said. "Q said it himself. He's the Snatcher. Why else would he be out this late, here of all places? Another coincidence, like when Mr. Arpin just 'ran' into him?"

"But he wasn't what grabbed Quinn back there."

"No," Hector said. "But that doesn't mean he's not in cahoots with whatever that was."

"Come out from there!" The rabbi roared. "Last warning!"

"Quinn, what do we do?"

He dared another peek. The rabbi was edging closer, his massive frame casting a wide shadow on the pine trees behind him.

Quinn's stomach lurched as the rabbi picked up Martin's lighter.

There it goes, he thought. *Our evidence.*

Right in the hands of the man who Quinn suspected all along.

Hector nudged him. "Quinn?" He gestured a little ways down the path.

Their bikes were just down the trail. With any luck, the rabbi hadn't seen them hidden in the bushes.

And they were covered in mud. Even with the lantern, they might be able to get by the rabbi without him recognizing them.

"We make a break for it," Quinn said. "RUN!"

As one, the Crypt Crew bounded onto the trail, sprinting as fast as their legs could carry them. The rabbi let out a cry as they sped by. He flailed wildly, trying to catch them as they passed. Quinn ducked down, narrowly missing the rabbi's hand swiping the neck of his shirt. He stumbled, skinning his knee on the gravel. Letting out a hiss of pain, he forced himself up as the rabbi lunged toward him, accidentally kicking off his mud-soaked boot. By then he didn't care, and ran with one bare foot all the way to the waiting bikes.

The Crew pedaled furiously down the access road, casting frenzied glances back to the trail, where the rabbi's lantern light faded into the darkness, his shouts lost behind the roar of the Falls.

Back at Quinn's, they each took turns blasting each other with freezing cold water from the hose until they were mostly cleansed of the mud and clay. Even so, Hector and Wendy would have to be extra careful sneaking back into their houses.

"Get out of those as quick as you can. And hide them."

"No problem," Hector said. "My mom calls my room the laundry mountain, anyway. She'll never find them."

"I do all of ours," Wendy said. "So I should be okay." She paused, looking at Quinn's house. "What about you? What will you tell Henry?"

Quinn shook his head. "I don't know. That lighter was our proof. Now that the rabbi has it...I'm not sure I can convince Henry to check out those caves again."

"We'll find a way," she told him. "People will have to start taking us seriously. We almost lost you tonight." Her hands balled to fists. "I'm not losing anyone. Not to this *thing*."

"Me neither," Hector said.

"Agreed. But for now, let's try to not get grounded by the morning. We'll meet back at Malman's. Maybe get some more clues together. You never know."

When Hector and Wendy left, Quinn quietly snuck back inside. He tiptoed down the hallway, careful not to step on the creaky spots. Before he went into his room, he paused, listening to muffled sounds from Henry's room. He was in the fit of another nightmare.

Quinn threw off his soaked clothes and collapsed onto his bed, dreading his own nightmares. Nightmares of man-eating clay creatures in deep caverns, and spooky rabbis lurking on dark forest paths.

Statues of Clay

Frantic pounding at the front door roused Quinn from a troubled sleep. As he stumbled into the hallway, Henry was buttoning up his shirt, already in his uniform, his face grim. Quinn looked at the clock on the wall. Just past five in the morning.

Quinn followed him. The bangs were so forceful he was surprised their door hadn't been knocked down.

"I'm coming!" Henry called over the ruckus. "Q, stand away, alright pal?"

Quinn positioned himself behind the couch as Henry swung the door open.

"Henry, thank God!"

It was Mr. Arpin. His oil-stained coveralls were slicked in wet clay.

"Jacques? What happened? Come inside."

"No time. You need to come with me. Need to see what I found."

"What you found?"

"The town green," he shook his head, his eyes squinting shut, like he was trying to shake some bad thought out of his head. "Will you come? Please? Before the whole town wakes up and sees? It's bad, Henry. Real bad."

Henry had told him to stay indoors, but as soon as he pulled away with Mr. Arpin, Quinn raced to the side of the house and hopped on his bike, following as best he could.

In the dewy dawn light, he watched as Henry, Mr. Arpin, and a few other people stood in a circle on the green. Mr. Malman was there, as was Mr. Harwich, scribbling furiously in his notebook, and, unfortunately, Mrs. Ruane, pacing and listening intently with her ear trumpet.

"Unacceptable!" she wailed. "Horrible! Would you just look at this *mess*?!"

Mr. Malman saw Quinn and shuffled over to him before he could get any closer.

"I don't think you want to see this," he told him. "Please, Quinn. Why don't you head over to the store?" He turned back to the onlookers. "I have a feeling this will draw quite the crowd. Might as well open for business."

Mr. Malman tried to stop him, but Quinn shouldered his way past and into the small circle.

There, beside the statue of Nathaniel Stark, stood two figures covered in clay.

Randall Colburn and Martin Ward were entombed in the stuff, frozen in place.

Both of their mouths hung open in silent screams, eyes wide in terror. Their arms were extended, Randall's reaching up, Martin's in front like he was fending something off.

"Horrid," Mrs. Ruane was saying over and over. "Just horrid."

Mr. Arpin nodded. "You think they're still...you know...alive?"

"Don't know, Jacques. That's a good question." Henry got on the radio. "Mabel? I need Doctor Delgado down at the green." He looked back at Randall and Martin. "And notify the funeral home."

"Alright, Deputy," Harwich said, "I think it's time you spilled. Who are your top suspects?"

Henry fixed the journalist with a cold glare.

"What the heck is going on out there, Henry?" Mabel's voice squeaked over the radio.

"Found Randall and Martin," he told her. "Snatcher left them right where the whole town can get a good gander."

There was a moment of silence. "Oh, my."

"Oh my is right," Henry said. "I'm gonna need some more manpower down here pretty soon. Can you see if Dale Francis is up?"

"Will do, Deputy."

"We need to move them," Mrs. Ruane said. "We can't have them displayed like this for everyone to see! It's sick!"

"Not until the doctor takes a look. This is a crime scene, Mrs. Ruane."

She scowled at that. "This whole town is a crime scene, apparently. Fine. Leave them here all you like, Deputy. They're killing the grass, you know."

Henry removed his hat.

"Jacques, you think you can fit them on the bed of the tow truck?"

"I'm on it," he said.

Harwich shook his notebook. "You still haven't divulged any details! This town deserves to know!"

Mrs. Ruane bristled beside the newspaperman. "Indeed!"

Watching from the bandstand, Quinn braced himself when he saw the look in Henry's eyes. When his brother spoke, his voice was deathly calm, the words coming from behind clenched teeth.

"Ma'am, these two men were my friends. Now I'm going to ask very nicely that you vacate the area and give me some space."

"Pardon?" she said, adjusting the ear trumpet.

"I think you heard me just fine." He turned to Harwich. "And you. Get back to your office. I'll have Mabel call as soon as she can."

Mrs. Ruane turned up her nose and strode off. Harwich followed soon after, dejected.

Alone for a few brief seconds, Quinn watched Henry place his hands on the two statues of his friends.

"I'm sorry, guys," he heard him say. "Sorry I couldn't find you in time."

Quinn's heart sank.

Henry turned away and spotted Quinn.

"And you. I thought I told you to stay put."

"I couldn't," he said. "You know I couldn't."

Henry shook his head. "Wish you could, though. Just stay out of the way, alright pal? This place is gonna be a madhouse in a few minutes."

And it was.

Before long, Dr. Delgado was on the scene, her medical bag slung over her shoulder as she walked around the statues, listening with stethoscopes and gently prodding with reflex hammers.

Half the town was crowded on either side of Main Street, watching from shop fronts and sidewalks.

"Dead?" Henry asked.

"No heartbeats." Hector's mom stepped back, furrowing her brow. "If I had to guess, I'd say they died by asphyxiation. Choked to death on the clay. Or it was poured on molten and they went into shock."

Quinn and Henry both winced.

As Dr. Delgado continued to examine the statues, Jacques Arpin's tow truck rumbled to a stop. The large man got out of his car, angrily slamming the door shut.

"Well," he said, "we won't be taking them to the county hospital anytime soon."

"And why's that?" Henry asked.

Jacques slipped his thumbs under the armpits of his coveralls and spat. "Bridge is out. Not even out. It's *gone*. Looks like something just ripped it right in half. Saw it when I pulled out of the garage."

"Old Rickety?"

Jacques nodded. "Irons all twisted up. Looks like a storm took out some of the supports. But we haven't had any bad weather. The thing is smashed to pieces."

Quinn watched Henry and Dr. Delgado's expressions drop.

The bridge was the main way in or out of the town, passing over Stark River and connecting to the highway. If it was damaged...

No way out.

While Henry got on the radio, Dr. Delgado called for Mr. Gibbs, the town mortician. The tiny man broke from the crowd of spectators, looking pale and frightened.

"We have a problem," Dr. Delgado told him. "My clinic is too small to do what needs doing. Can we take them to your morgue?"

The mortician balked at the statues, then back to Dr. Delgado. "Of course," he said. "But what are you planning to do?"

"I need to cut into them," she said in a low voice. "See how exactly they died. How the Snatcher or whatever we're calling him managed to do this."

"The morgue's at your disposal, Doc."

"Thanks, Gibbs. Jacques, I'm going to need to hoist them up on your truck. Think you can manage that?"

"Anything for you," Mr. Arpin said.

"Alright," Henry said, closing the car door. "I told Mabel to get a message out to the State PD and Public Works about that bridge. It'll probably be a week before they send a repair crew. Maybe a bit longer."

"Folks aren't gonna take it well," Mr. Arpin said.

"The only way in or out? With a killer on the loose? I know, Jacques."

"Well," the big man said, "It's not the only way."

The Park Ranger truck rolled onto the green beside the Sheriff's car. Wendy and her dad emerged.

Quinn whistled to Wendy while her dad joined the group. They sat on the bandstand while Henry filled Mr. Francis in.

"There's the old logger's path through the mountain," Mr. Francis said, "but it's been a while since I checked on it. Could be rough going."

"There's the hunting trails," Mr. Arpin offered. "Old ones the French trappers used back when my folks were running around these parts. Even so, it would be slow going. Elmwood is eighteen, nineteen miles south. That's a lot of ground to cover on foot, and hard hiking."

Mr. Gibbs wrung his hands. "So we're trapped? Truly?"

All eyes fell on Henry.

He took off his hat, wringing it in his hands as he paced in front of the men trapped in clay.

"Yes. Cars won't make it out of here, Stanley. People can try on foot, but..." he paused, frowning. "I don't think that's a good idea. The river's too wide and rapid, can't expect folks to try and swim for it, even ford it. It narrows about twenty or so miles down, but again, no roads." He sighed. "We *are* trapped. And I think that's what the Snatcher wanted all along." He turned to the others. "I'm calling a town meeting."

"He's got us like fish in a barrel," Mr. Francis said.

Mr. Arpin nodded with another yank on his coveralls. "And if one fish tries to swim away on its own..."

"Easy pickings for the Snatcher," Dr. Delgado finished.

"Well," Mr. Gibbs said shakily, "In the words of Mr. Shakespeare, we are in a pickle, aren't we?"

"Sure are," Henry said. "Biggest pickle I've ever seen."

Behind them, the petrified bodies of Randall and Martin stared out with fear-filled eyes, issuing silent screams.

Quinn stared at them with the eerie sense that any second, one of them would move. But he'd heard it from Dr. Delgado herself.

The men were dead.

Henry's best friends, who'd looked after Quinn like a little brother.

"We need to find what did this," Wendy said. "We need to go back to the caves."

"But this time we'll be prepared," Quinn said. He thought about the rabbi. There was no way he'd just happened to be walking by in the middle of the night. One way or another, he'd find out what Rabbi Shwartz knew. Then he'd have what he needed to stop the Snatcher for good

Quinn jumped down from the bandstand, taking one last look as Henry and Jacques secured Randall's body to the truck.

"Henry," he heard Mr. Arpin say in a low voice, "about the Old Rickety..."

Henry looked at him, his face drawn and tired. "What about the bridge?"

"Didn't want to upset the rest of the folks, but...the thing was covered in clay."

The words froze Quinn in his tracks.

He stared into the statue's eyes. The last thing Randall had ever seen, would ever see, was the mysterious creature that'd done this to him.

Quinn shuddered at the thought.

When he did, Randall's eye moved, swirling around in its socket. It fixed on him.

Quinn gasped.

"What is it?" Wendy asked.

Mr. Arpin started the truck and slowly drove across the green towards Gibb's Funeral Home. Quinn tried to catch another glimpse of Randall, but the whole scene was lost in a haze of diesel smoke.

"His eyes," Quinn said.

"Huh?"

He swallowed, feeling like he had a stone lodged in his throat.

"Let's go," Wendy said. "Hector's waiting at Malman's. Tell me later, okay?"

The Morgue

Malman and Son's was packed. Most of the town was wide-awake and crowding Main Street. Quinn could barely hear himself think over the frantic conversations as he and Wendy wound their way through the aisles.

They found Hector sitting on the floor by the bookstand, surrounded by comics and horror magazines. He was flipping through an issue of *The Horror Vault*, pouring over the pages intensely as if he were studying for a math test.

"Hector?" Wendy said, taking a seat next to him.

Hector didn't look up. He flipped another page, his forehead covered in a light sheen of sweat.

"It's gotta be here," he said quietly. "Something solid. Something we can use." He tossed aside the *Vault* and picked up an old *Tales From the Crypt*. "There has to be something."

"Okay," Quinn said, crouching down in front of him. "Hector, what's the matter?"

He finally looked up. "The matter? We ran—" he stopped himself, looking around the crowded store, lowering his voice. "We ran into a monster last night. A real, bona fide monster. I'm trying to find out what it is." He held up the magazine. "You know, I think we've been looking at these wrong. They're not just stories and neat pictures. We can use this stuff. Like a manual. A monster hunting manual!"

Quinn looked down at the comic book. A grave robber was making his way into a rat-infested tunnel. He carried a lantern and shovel, face twisted in an evil grin. Quinn couldn't help but conjure an image of Rabbi Shwartz.

"We know it's nocturnal," Hector said. "So it could be a vampire. But vampires don't turn people into statues."

"Medusa!" Wendy said. "She did. If you looked her in the eyes, you got turned to stone."

Quinn thought about the thing in the tunnel, how strong it had been, the strange hand crushing his ankle like a vice.

"But she doesn't have super strength," Hector said. "This thing can crush cars and fit into small spaces. Gorgons can't do that...I don't think."

"Maybe it's a shapeshifter. Like some kind of demon."

Quinn wracked his brain, going through every possible monster he could think of. Zombies, werewolves, possessed dolls, goblins and trolls and ghosts, crazed killers and murderous aliens. Nothing fit the bill. The thing that grabbed him in the cave wasn't like anything he'd read about. Or even wrote about. There was a part of him, a very small part, that thought this would make a great story. If they lived long enough to write it, at least.

"Kids!"

Mr. Malman walked into the aisle, looking haggard.

"Think you can come help me up at the counter?"

Quinn and Wendy were put on bagging duty while Hector helped at the register. Each customer they rang up had a different theory.

"It's that Brent Foster," Tom Castelot, the owner of the textile mill said. "Never been right since his accident at the mill. Lives all alone out past the Falls."

"Hmm," Mr. Malman said thoughtfully, as he did with every customer. "I'd have Deputy Katz check on that, Tom."

He scoffed. "That kid? He can barely tie his own shoes, far as I'm concerned. Plus him and Brent go way back. You think he'd turn in his buddy? I don't care how many times they throw that 'hero' word around when it comes to Henry Katz. Let's hope old Toohey gets back soon."

As soon as the words left his mouth, he spotted Quinn. Tom's face reddened. "Sorry there, son. No hard feelings, you see, it's just—"

Mr Malman coughed. "Thanks, Tom. You take care now." He put the money in Mr. Castelot's hands with extra force.

"I apologize," Mr. Castelot said. "But this whole bridge business could ruin us! I'll have to halt production, which means most of the town is out of work. No lumber in or out. No textiles. No supplies. No mail. This is bad, Jonas."

"We've seen hard times," Mr. Malman said.

"Not like this," the mill owner said, wiping a hand across his brow. "Not with a killer on the loose and no way out. My son's having nightmares. Kid usually sleeps like the dead. Not anymore. Wakes up screaming about globs of clay chasing him."

As he walked away, Mr. Malman sighed. "Sorry about that, Quinn. Maybe you should be over at the soda counter."

"That's okay," Quinn said.

People will always talk, he thought. *Even if they don't have anything helpful to say.*

Two teenagers were next in line. Emily Swinburn and Deborah Locke.

"We were supposed to go to the drive in," Emily was saying, "Pete promised to take me to see *The Fog*. Now our plans are ruined!"

"Well *I* was supposed to visit my cousins in Bangor this weekend," Debbie said. "You think I want to be stuck here?"

"I'm sure the bridge will be fixed in no time," Mr. Malman said assuredly.

"I hope you're right, Mr. Malman," Emily said. "My Dad says it better be, or else we'll all wind up like Randall and Martin."

"I doubt that very much," he said, ringing up their items. "We're going to be just fine. You'll see."

The girls gave him skeptical glances as Quinn handed them their bags.

On and on, it went. Mostly people complained about the bridge, or threw out names of suspects. After an hour, Quinn figured the list was about as big as the town itself. But that's what happened when you lived in a place like Stark Falls, and everyone knew everyone.

The bell over the door jingled as Terry Pots, Frank Castelot, and Maria entered wearing heavy overcoats. Quinn eyed them suspiciously. It was almost ninety-five degrees outside.

"Rabbi Shwartz," Hector said. "It has to be him. Right, guys?"

Three Garden Club women in line stiffened at that. They huddled in close, whispering.

"I knew it!" Quinn heard Terry whisper to Frank.

Mr. Malman bristled.

Once the next customers were taken care of, he spun around on Hector.

"And what, Mr. Delgado," he snapped, "would compel you to make an accusation like that?"

Hector took a step back, shocked at Mr. Malman's tone.

"Well, it's just—"

"It's just *nothing*!" He motioned for Quinn and Wendy to join him. "Let me tell you something about our nice little town, kids. Something I think you need to learn sooner rather than later." He looked over his shoulder to make sure no one was near the counter.

"When bad things happen, people look for someone to blame. A scapegoat. Someone they don't trust. Someone they don't think belongs." He lowered his voice. "Rabbi Shwartz is a good man, who's done more for me than anyone else. Quinn, you of all people should know how dangerous it would be if these people thought it was the *rabbi* doing something like this."

Quinn balked at that. "Me? Why?"

"Think about it, son. Stark Falls isn't exactly a melting pot. Besides you, Mrs. Epstein, me, and your brother, the rabbi is the only other Jew in the entire town, now that Randall's gone. There's maybe twenty of us in the whole County."

"So?" Hector asked. "What's that got to do with anything?"

"Everything," Mr. Malman said. "Kids, you may not notice it, and that's a good thing, but people in this town are wary of anything different from themselves."

"Like me," Wendy said. "Because of my mom."

Mr. Malman's face was pained. "Yes, Wendy. Because of your

mother. It's disgusting, but true. People will always be suspicious of those who don't live like them, or talk like them, or go to the same church."

"So because I'm Jewish and Wendy's parents don't live together, we can't make our own guesses?"

"No, no, no," Mr. Malman said, exasperated. "I'm saying that *because* of those things, you need to be careful what you say, and what you do. A lot more careful than most kids."

"That's wrong," Hector said. "My mom says we should be proud of who we are."

"You should be," Malman said. "Your mother is an extraordinary woman."

The Crew looked at one another, confused.

"This isn't coming out right," Malman said. "And it sure isn't a conversation I'd planned on having this soon. But I want you to understand that the world doesn't play fair. Not for people like us. When people get riled up, they look for someone to blame. Someone different. Time and again, they do it, from ancient history until now." His face darkened. "Even people like my boy, who make the ultimate sacrifice. So it's very important in times like these that we stick together and keep quiet. I don't want to hear any more talk about the rabbi like that, understood?"

The kids nodded.

"There's plenty of nice things about Stark Falls. Plenty of good people. Truly good people. I don't want to make it seem like this is a bad place. I just want you to know how people think. People like us, we need to behave a certain way, because if we don't…"

"Bad things can happen," Wendy said.

"But Mr. Malman," Hector said, "what if there's a really good reason for thinking he did it?"

"Hector, please. I can't hear it. I won't."

Quinn saw the pain in Malman's eyes.

A part of him always knew he was different. They all were. The Crypt Crew *existed* because they were different. But he never really thought about how the rest of the town saw them. Terry Pots and Frank Castelot and the rest of their gang gave them grief, sure, but nothing serious. Surely it wasn't everybody, but enough that Mr. Malman thought it important enough to give them a crash course in racism and small town ignorance.

As he watched Malman tiredly man the register, he realized that Rabbi Shwartz was the only person who had really been there for him after Ethan died. Every night, they'd study the Torah and eat together. The rabbi was Malman's only comfort in life, aside from the store.

Of course he doesn't want it to be the rabbi, he thought. *Because if it is, he'd lose his only friend.*

Quinn decided they shouldn't bring it up anymore. At least not where Malman could hear them.

"Remember what I said," he told them. "It's important that we stick together. All of us. I have a feeling things will get much worse before they get better."

"Are you going to the meeting?" Quinn asked. He looked out the window, where a crowd was already gathering at Town Hall.

"Me? No. Plenty of stuff to do here." Malman glanced to the cellar door. "Inventory."

A loud *clang* echoed from the basement storage room.

"Boiler trouble again?"

Malman ran a hand over his face. "It seems I'm cursed." He smiled. "But if all I'm cursed with is a bum boiler, I guess it's not so bad, far as curses go, huh kids? All right, off you go. Thanks for all your help today, and tell your folks I said hello."

Quinn looked out over the town green, where lines of caution tape marked off the crime scene. They needed to find the Snatcher, and fast.

If they couldn't, there'd be a lot more statues before long.

"Weird," Hector said.

"What's that?"

"The rabbi. Did you guys see him at all today?"

Wendy and Quinn shook their heads.

First the fireworks, now this.

"He's up to something," Hector said. "Malman just doesn't want to see it."

"Whatever he's doing, we'll find out," Quinn told him.

One way or another.

"MAKE A RUN FOR IT!"

Terry, Frank, and Maria bolted towards the door. Their unseasonable winter coats were bulky, and they *clanged* and *crinkled* as the trio ran.

"Shoplifters!" Hector cried.

"Eat my boxers, monster geek!" Terry yelled over his shoulder. He looked back and sneered at Hector. Behind him, Frank let out a huge guffaw. Quinn thought he sounded like a horse.

Wendy jumped over the counter, sprinting to the door.

Still laughing, Terry ran headfirst into a shelf of pickles, sending jars smashing against the ground. The entire general store suddenly stank of vinegar. Terry slipped, landing hard on his backside. Frank, still neighing like a cartoon horse, didn't notice and went skidding across the floor, slamming into Mrs. Ruane's apple dolls. He fell down on a bunch of them with a *splat*.

Maria took the lead, struggling to keep her coat from unbuttoning under the extra bulk.

"Stop!" Hector said. "Stop right now!"

Wendy reached the door and turned the deadbolt.

"Move it," Maria said.

Wendy crossed her arms.

"Not until you put everything back."

"Yeah," Hector said. "And apologize to Mr. Malman."

"And pay for the stuff you just broke," Wendy said, nodding to Terry and Frank, both moaning in pain as they picked themselves up.

Maria bristled.

Quinn and Hector moved to join Wendy, the three of them blocking the door.

"Maria, please," Quinn said. "Just put it down, alright?"

Her eyes narrowed. Quinn tensed, remembering the nasty bruise she'd given Hector. He recoiled, trying to stop his heart from beating so fast. He'd never fight a girl, he thought, and especially not Maria. He doubted he'd last five seconds.

"Fine," she snapped. She unbuttoned her coat, letting the stolen goods fall to the floor. Quinn saw canned food, a fire starter, some lamp oil, bug spray, and tons of candy hit the ground.

"You too," Wendy called to the boys. Terry and Frank shared a miserable look, and let their stuff out of their jackets. More candy, along with a pair of sunglasses, a blanket, a small tarp, flashlights and a mosquito net.

"What's this for?" Quinn asked.

Maria let out a loud huff, wiping some stray strands of hair from her face.

"We're going camping," she said.

"For Nature Scouts," Terry chimed in, soaked in pickle vinegar.

"Yeah, right," Wendy said. "My Dad's Scout Leader, remember? You guys aren't having your first camping trip till the end of the month."

"And you're not even allowed to be a Scout this summer," Hector said.

"Okay, okay," Maria said. "We're going to hike up the old logging trail and get some help, alright? No one else in this town has the guts to do it, especially not our Deputy." She shot Quinn a cold look.

"Yeah," Frank said, "So it's up to the Scouts to save the day."

"You do know there's a mon—" Hector caught himself, "a killer on the loose, right?"

"The Snowshoe Snatcher?" Maria snorted. "I think we'll be okay."

"Yeah," Terry said. "So long as we stay away from Rabbi Shwartz."

"He's the killer," Frank said, "You guys said so yourselves."

"And maybe you're his helper, right Katz? You people like to stick together, don't you?"

"You people?" Quinn felt the anger sear his veins. But the idea of fighting anyone made him sick, and he could feel his stomach churn with nausea.

"Look," Maria said, taking a step towards the Crypt Crew, "we dropped everything. Let us go."

Wendy looked to Quinn and Hector. Hector gave her a slight nod. The deadbolt clicked, and the door swung open.

"Wait," Hector said, blocking the way. "Not until you say sorry to Mr. Malman."

"Oh, right. You're best friend, the weirdo."

"He's not a weirdo."

"Takes one to know one."

"Maria, I'm telling Mom as soon as I get home. You're gonna be sorry."

Maria moved so quickly Hector had no time to react. She grabbed his arm, twisted it behind his back, and shoved him hard against the door. Hector let out a howl of pain as his elbow cracked against the doorframe.

Wendy stepped forward.

"You want the same?" Maria asked her. "Try me, Francis. I don't care who your dad is."

"Really? You think when he hears about this he won't kick you out of the Scouts?"

Maria flinched.

"Just get out of here," Wendy said, her voice dangerously low. "Now."

"Don't have to tell me twice!" Frank said, quickly abandoning his partners in crime.

Maria bent down. "If you tell Mom, I'll make this the worst summer of your life. Understand?"

Hector didn't reply. He curled into the fetal position, shielding his head.

"And you," she said to Wendy, an angry tear falling down her cheek. "Can go ahead and tell your dad that this is my idea. I'll show him and everyone else in this stupid town what I can do. You just watch!"

Quinn and Wendy parted, making room as the three ran out onto the sidewalk and disappeared around the corner.

Hector was curled up on the ground, crying as he cradled his elbow.

"Here," Wendy said, crouching down next to him, "let me see."

"It's bad," Hector said, sniffling. "Uh, oh."

"What? What is it?"

Quinn watched as Hector took his hand away from the elbow. Bright red blood stained his palm.

Oh, no.

"He doesn't do well with—"

"I think I'm gonna be sick," Hector said, groaning.

The basement door flew open.

"What in heaven's name is all this?" Mr. Malman cried, looking around wide-eyed.

"My sister," Hector began, then hissed in pain as he dabbed at the cut. "Ouch!"

"They tried to steal some stuff," Quinn said. "But Wendy and Hector stopped them."

"Who?" Mr. Malman's voice was very soft.

"Terry, Frank, and Maria. They're gonna try to hike the old logging trail through the mountain to get help."

Malman's jaw twitched. Quinn could practically see the anger seething. He wouldn't have been surprised if smoke started billowing from Malman's ears.

"Come on, Hector," he said, "let's get you cleaned up. You've got quite a cut, there."

"She got me good," Hector said as Wendy helped him up. His face was pale, and he kept his head turned away from the blood.

"Some apples are rotten," Mr. Malman said. "No matter how healthy the tree."

That's one way of putting it, Quinn thought as Malman fixed up Hector's cut with some iodine and a few bandages.

"There. Good as new." He stretched, spine popping as he raised his arms above his head. "Looks like I have my work cut out for me. This place will smell like pickles 'till September."

"We can stay and help," Wendy said.

"It's the least we can do," Quinn added.

Malman waved them off.

"No, no. You caught the bandits. Job well done. Leave the rest to me."

"You sure?" Hector asked.

"I'm sure. You just make sure your mother takes a look at that, okay? You may need stitches."

"I will." He hesitated, shifting awkwardly from side to side. "I'm sorry about my sister. She has anger problems, and she—"

"No need to explain," Mr. Malman said. "Siblings are difficult, sometimes. I'll handle the shoplifters. Don't you worry about that."

"We're sorry," Quinn said. "Really."

"You didn't do this," Mr. Malman said. "You have nothing to be sorry about. Why don't you three run along home? I'll be fine."

Henry's Town Hall meeting was scheduled for six o'clock. Not wanting the kids to have to sit through it, he called Dr. Delgado, who arranged for Quinn and Wendy to stay at her house with Hector. Luckily, Maria had called to say she was staying over Gail Trumbull's house. Hector decided to wait until his mom got home to tell her the truth. Quinn and Wendy agreed.

"They can't seriously be thinking of going out there alone," Wendy said.

"Maria loves the Nature Scouts," Hector replied. "That's why she's so angry all the time. Because of summer school. She's trying to prove she can do it."

"Yeah," Wendy said. "By getting herself kicked out of the Scouts altogether, once my dad finds out."

"I didn't say it's a good idea," Hector said. He gingerly poked at his bandaged elbow. "Anyway, I hope they don't. That's about the stupidest thing I can think of. Maria's smarter than those other kids. She should know better."

"I wish she didn't hurt you like that," Wendy said.

"Well," Hector sighed. "She's hurt, too. She just shows it different, is all." He shifted uncomfortably, clutching his bandaged hand.

"I'm sure they won't go," Quinn said. "We made them drop all their supplies."

Hector nodded, seeming to ease a bit.

"You're right," he said. "She and Gail will probably just have a slumber party. Which gives me a break. One night, at least."

They'd set up in Hector's basement, continuing their search for clues inside his hidden stash of horror comics. On the television, *The Black Scorpion* was playing on *Nightmare Theater*. Every now and then the Crew would pause to watch giant insects terrorize a small Mexican village.

After a particularly gruesome scene, Quinn decided to finally tell them about Randall Colburn's eyes.

"Tell me again," Hector said. "*Exactly* what you saw."

"He stared right at me," Quinn said. "I'm telling you guys, he was still alive in there."

"Or he could be changed," Wendy said. "You know…risen, like a zombie."

"Or a vampire's thrall," Hector added, his face paling.

"He didn't look like that to me," Quinn said, thinking back. The look in Randall's eyes had been frightened, pleading.

"So they're still alive," Hector said. "And they can't move." His brows raised. He bolted off the couch. "Guys! My mom's gonna cut them open!"

"We can't let that happen," Wendy said. "Quinn, you *sure* you saw?"

He nodded. He'd seen some strange things, lately. Things that he would usually chalk up to daydreams or nightmares. But Randall's eyes were real. As real as the thing that pulled him into the mud.

"We need to get into the funeral home," he said. "Any ideas?"

"I have one," Hector said.

They followed him up into the kitchen, where he grabbed a set of brass skeleton keys from a bowl. "Mr. Gibbs left these with her. She said she's going to start work on them tomorrow."

"And what about Gibbs?"

"He's at the meeting with everyone else,"

"Abbie?"

Hector shrugged. "Probably over at someone's house. Maybe Clark's. And if not, I don't think she'll be hanging around the, you know." He held out his arms straight and walked like The Mummy. "Where they keep the stiffs."

This was their chance. Probably the only one they'd ever have. If Randall and Martin were alive, they needed to make sure.

"Okay," Quinn said, "But we get this done fast. In and out. No trouble."

T hey slowed their bikes as they pulled onto the sidewalk of Main Street. A long line of cars was parked at the curb, with more crowding the small parking lot at Town Hall. Quinn glanced up and down the street. All the shops had closed early. The rows of gabled colonial houses stood eerily shadowed, not a light in a single window. His gaze lingered on Malman's for a while.

"You think it's true," Hector asked, "all that stuff Malman was saying? About being, you know, different?"

"Part of it," Wendy said.

Quinn silently agreed.

For the most part, the Crypt Crew was left alone. But even that was part of it. They were kept away from things by the other kids. Shunned. Out of the inner circle. Aside from Abbie and Clark, that is. Quinn knew that if he didn't have Wendy and Hector, his life would be a hard one. And lonely.

A part of him knew that's why the Crypt Crew loved monsters so much. They were neat, sure. But there was another aspect of monsters that they could relate to. Quinn, Hector, and Wendy felt a *kinship* with the monsters of legends and movies and books. They, too, were lonely and misunderstood. Always kept at arm's length. Never welcomed in. They weren't all bad. Some were gentle, but pushed into situations that caused them to lash out. In a way, many monsters were sad.

But the monster lurking around Stark Falls was anything but.

"I think he was right," Quinn said. "But we have to remember that Mr. Malman is, well,"

"Different?"

"Not himself," Quinn said. "Not since Ethan."

"It's getting to him, if you ask me," Hector said. "And I don't care what he says. It all points to Rabbi Shwartz."

"It looks that way," Quinn said. He paused. "But—"

"But we can't be sure," Wendy finished for him.

"Let's hurry before that meeting lets out," Hector said. "I don't want to see Randall and Martin cut into like Thanksgiving turkeys."

The Gibbs Funeral Home stood on the corner of Main Street and Dekker Avenue, facing the town green. Town Hall was just across the way. Quinn could make out people moving behind the windows and wondered how Henry was handling himself. Judging by the number of cars parked up and down the street, most of the town had shown up. That meant a few hundred scared, angry people crammed into a single room, demanding answers.

He didn't envy his brother. He was sure Hampton Harwich was leading the charge, screaming accusations, and raising questions. While

Henry kept the people of Stark Falls at bay, the Crypt Crew would help as best they could.

"It's around back," Hector said, leading them around the side of the funeral home. "Mom's used this place a few times. The morgue is in the basement."

"You've been inside?" Wendy asked.

Hector balked at that. "Me? No way. Mom never let me go in. But that doesn't mean I never peeked." He gestured to a leaded window, which gave a small, blurry view into the lit basement. Quinn and Wendy crouched down, but the only thing visible was a metal table with an odd assortment of tools.

"Here," Wendy said, handing Quinn the keys.

"Why me?"

"You're the one who saw the statue come to life," she said matter-of-factly. "That makes you the mission leader."

"I'll be the lookout," Hector offered, nervously scratching the back of his neck with his bandaged hand. "I mean, all three of us don't have to go inside. I can be more useful out here. You know, in case the meeting lets out early. I'll yodel."

"Or bark like a dog?" Wendy asked.

Quinn knew Hector had been shaken pretty bad by what happened inside the cave. Not to mention his latest scrape with Maria. His normal "macho man" persona was missing. "Good idea. Wendy and I can go inside and look around. If anyone comes, give a loud whistle."

Hector saluted and crept over to the corner of the building, watching Town Hall.

Quinn's pulse quickened as he inserted the key into the lock. Last night, they'd snuck into a place they shouldn't have. But this was different. This was breaking the law. Quinn shuddered at the thought of Henry catching them. He paused, the key half-turned in the lock.

"What is it?"

"Just thinking about my brother," he said. "What he'd say if he could see us right now."

Wendy put a hand on his shoulder. "We're doing this to help him," she said. "To help the whole town. And Randall and Martin." She looked over to where Hector was keeping watch. "And we don't have a lot of time. So what do you say? Ready to become Stark Falls' Dr. Van Helsing?"

Quinn looked around the alley, took a deep breath, and turned the key. Quietly, he and Wendy walked down the metal stairs and into the gloom of the embalming room.

A strange scent filled Quinn's nostrils.

The embalming fluid, he figured. He'd read plenty of stories that took place in morgues and mortuaries, and there was always mention of embalming fluid. Horror writers loved to talk about the stuff. He'd never actually smelled any until now, and it made him slightly dizzy. Wendy held her nose shut, moving slowly past the tables and workbenches.

Quinn studied the metal saws, hammers, and clamps, like salad tongs but with sharp points at the ends. Scalpels and tubes, and something that looked like a turkey baster attached to a hose also caught his attention. There were also tons of makeup tools. Flesh-colored paint, fake eyelashes, even hairpieces.

"I think this is them," Wendy said, stopping by two metal doors set in the wall. Quinn opened one, pulling out the metal slab on rollers. On top of the slab was a body bag, zipped up tight. A rush of cool air followed, stale with a hint of cleaning solution.

Carefully, he drew down the zipper until Randall's clay-encrusted face was exposed.

"What do we do now?" Wendy asked.

Quinn studied Randall, looking for any movement in the eyes.

"How about that?" He pointed to a hammer. On one side was something that looked like a chisel. He guessed it was for breaking bone and decided it would work just as well on clay.

Wendy handed it to him, looking worriedly at Randall's face.

Quinn unzipped the body bag further until Randall's chest was exposed. He held the hammer up, aiming it just above the rib cage. It wasn't going to be a heavy blow. Just enough to chip away the clay until he could reach the skin.

"I need to get some of the clay out of the way," he told her. "So I can see if his heart is still beating."

"Just be careful," she said. "If you hit him too hard, he might crumble."

Quinn looked up at her. She shrugged. "You never know."

"Okay," he said. "Gentle taps. Just to be safe."

He raised the hammer.

A loud whistle came from the window.

"Guys!" Hector's muffled voice was dulled by the thick glass. "Guys, get out of there!"

Faint footsteps thudded overhead.

"Quick!" Hector yelled. "*Ruff*! *Ruff*!"

"He actually *did* it!" Wendy whispered.

Quinn quickly zipped up Randall's body bag and pushed the slab back into the wall.

A door creaked open at the top of the stairs.

"Psst!" Wendy hissed, gesturing to a metal tub with a lid. It was big enough for them both to fit inside, like a large freezer. Quinn followed her in, thankful it wasn't actually a freezer, and hunkered down. Two small holes from the lid's hinges gave him a limited view of the room, and just as Wendy closed it on top of them, he saw Mr. Gibbs descending the stairs. The mortician was quiet as a mouse, and walked with delicate, soft steps. If Hector hadn't warned them, Quinn and Wendy might not have heard him at all.

A second, much louder pair of feet followed Gibbs down into the morgue. Quinn saw large boots caked in mud. The heavy limp was unmistakable.

Rabbi Shwartz came into view. His tangled mane of gray hair was wilder than ever. He looked like he hadn't slept in a week.

"What's he doing here?" Wendy whispered.

Quinn could only stare, straining his sight through the small pinpoint of vision the metal tub allowed him. The two men paused at the refrigerated compartments. Gibbs paused, his hands hovering over the bars.

"You're sure about this?" The mortician asked. "I mean, no offense, rabbi, but this is highly unusual. Doctor Delgado hasn't even examined them yet."

"Mr. Gibbs," Rabbi Shwartz growled, "Everything about this is highly unusual. Please, if you would." He gestured to the door.

Pale, Gibbs opened the door nervously.

"You said Deputy Katz is alright with this?"

Quinn tensed at his brother's name.

"Fine, just fine," The rabbi said, sounding impatient.

"I just wasn't aware the Sheriff was using…uh…members of the community to help in all this."

"I'd appreciate it," Rabbi Shwartz said, "if you kept this visit between us. No one else needs to know, including the good Doctor."

Gibbs nodded a bit too vigorously. Quinn could see the poor man was flustered, scared half to death.

The Rabbi unzipped the body bag and leaned in close.

Gibbs watched over the enormous man's shoulder.

"What are you, um, looking for, exactly?"

The rabbi slowly walked around Randall's body, muttering something very quietly under his breath.

"Beg pardon?" Mr. Gibbs asked.

"It's Hebrew," the Rabbi said. "I'm…praying, Mr. Gibbs."

"Ah," the undertaker said with relief. "That's nice. Although Mr. Ward over there is Episcopalian. We go to the same church."

"Fascinating," the Rabbi replied dryly.

"You, uh, never told me what you're looking for," Gibbs pressed.

"Markings."

"I see. Signs of a struggle? Things like that?"

"No."

The rabbi made another slow round of the body, softly chanting something under his breath.

"What's he doing?" Wendy asked quietly.

Quinn shook his head, knowing she couldn't see him, and continued to stare at the odd scene. The rabbi nodded, Gibbs put Randall away, and the whole process started over for Martin.

Quinn's legs and neck were beginning to cramp. He tried to adjust himself, but was too afraid to move in the tub, worried about making the slightest noise.

"Find anything?" Gibbs asked.

"Nothing that I'm looking for," the Rabbi said, his tone cryptic. "I think I'm done here. Thank you, Gibbs. You've been a big help."

"Anything to be of service," Gibbs said, his voice a tad too high and squeaky. "Give my best to the Deputy."

The Rabbi paused, staring at the man for some time before giving a brisk nod.

Quinn kept his eyes on Gibbs, who let out a deep breath as the heavy boots ascended the staircase. His spine felt like a corkscrew. He wondered how long they'd have to stay crammed in a metal box in the morgue.

Once the rabbi was gone, Mr. Gibbs turned on the radio and went to the other side of the room, out of Quinn's view.

A loud click drifted through the morgue followed by a whirring sound.

"July Eighth," Gibbs said, "Two bodies discovered on the town green. Both male, early twenties. Randall Colburn and Martin Ward. Bodies fully encased in hardened clay. This is…extraordinarily odd, to say the least. Acting Medical Examiner for the case is Inez Delgado, M.D. Deputy Henry Katz and myself will also be participating in the autopsy, scheduled for tomorrow afternoon. Needless to say, I'm a bit overwhelmed. Never, in my thirty years working in this town, have I come across something so…". Quinn listened as the tape recorder whirred in the cold, sterile room. "*Evil.*"

He spoke that last word with a measure of fear that Quinn had never heard an adult utter.

"That's all for tonight. I might make some notes before the autopsy. Checking the bodies now. More out of curiosity than anything else."

A click, and the recorder fell silent.

Rick "Madman" Wade's voice echoed through the room. Quinn thought his smooth tones sounded wildly out of place.

"Bit of news," he said, "just came through the wire. The bridge in Stark Falls is out. Chalked up to a freak accident. Road traffic is closed until further notice. How's that for bad luck? No way in or out, unless someone has a plane handy! Let's all send some positive thoughts to the folks in the Falls, huh? Reports of a so-called "Snowshoe Snatcher" stalking the area has been the talk of the county for a few days now. Any news, Stark Falls? If so, call in and let old Madman know you're safe and sound. I received another request from "Mr. Lonely". So here you go, you lonesome soul. Hope this helps."

The sound of a needle touching down on a record scraped its way through the speaker. A familiar song lilted into the room. As soon as the first few notes were sung, Quinn felt Wendy's fingers digging into his skin so hard his hand began to fall numb. The words that followed had seemed to haunt them ever since this whole mess began. The song that they'd come across too many times for it to be a coincidence, now.

When the night falls silently
  The night falls silently on forests dreaming

Mr. Gibbs opened the door, pulling Randall back out.

Lovers wander forth to see the bright stars gleaming

He unzipped the bag, donning a pair of gloves. He fixed a pair of magnifiers over his glasses.

And lest they should lose their way,
  The glow-worms nightly light their lanterns gay

He tilted Randall's head side to side, looking closely into the corpse's eyes.

Their tiny lanterns gay and twinkle brightly

Used a small reflex hammer and began tapping, his ears close to the body, tapping from the neck, down to the shoulders, down the arm...

Here and there and everywhere, from mossy dell and hollow
  Floating, gliding through the air, they call on us to follow...

Nodded, satisfied, and removed his gloves. He picked up a notepad, glancing at the clock on the wall before jotting something down.

Shine, little glow-worm, glimmer,
  Shine, little glow-worm, glimmer!
  Lead us, lest to far we wander
  Love's sweet voice is calling yonder

Wiped his hands on his coat, turning away to set the notepad down on the table.

Shine, little glow-worm, glimmer
  Shine, little glow-worm, glimmer!

A loud *creak* from the slab.
Gibbs turned.

Light the path below above

Randall sat up, bits of clay falling to the floor as he reached out and took Mr. Gibbs by the throat.

And lead us on to love!

Gibbs tried to scream, but all that came out was a gargled yelp. Randall's eyes moved in clay-caked sockets,. He stared at Gibbs, and Quinn saw his fist squeeze hard.

Shine, little glow-worm, glimmer! Glimmer!

Gibbs fell to the floor. Randall's head moved in taught, jerky motions. Movements a statue would make, Quinn thought, if one came to life. He set one leg on the floor. Wendy's grip tightened, and Quinn found himself gripping her just as tight.
Randall stood. Took a few steps, like Frankenstein's monster learning how to walk.
Gibbs was on the floor, gasping. Quinn could see the tips of his shoes before Randall stepped into full view. Clouds of clay dust followed as he stomped towards the other door. He reached out his stony hand, gripped the door handle and pulled the entire metal gurney out of the wall, sending the handle *clanging* to the ground.
Randall moved slowly. Deliberately. He unzipped Martin's body bag and stepped back. Soon, Martin lurched up. Their faces had changed. The whites of their eyes were a sickly yellow. Instead of frozen screams, they were both frowning. Stone faced. *Actually* stone faced.

"Uuuoooohhh," Mr. Gibbs moaned.

The two clay corpses looked down.

Gibbs kicked his feet, struggling to move.

Quinn bit his lip, stifling a scream.

Randall and Martin leaned over Gibbs. They opened their mouths wide.

Too wide.

Quinn thought they looked like a pair of snakes unhinging their jaws. Yet instead of swallowing Gibbs like the thought they would, they let out a loud, sickening belch. Mud and clay poured from their mouths, flowing like a waterfall. The smell was awful.

Gibbs coughed, legs kicking wildly as the sludge buried him. Quinn saw steam rise, and soon the smell was so bad he began to gag. Luckily, the music from the radio and the sound of the corpses spewing was loud enough to cover it up.

Martin turned to the radio, crushing it flat with a massive fist. In the silence that followed, Quinn heard Mr. Gibbs struggling, slipping and sliding, trying to slither his way out from under the mound of muck. Quinn remembered using clay in art class. He thought about how heavy even a smaller sized box of the stuff was. Gibbs was under pounds of it.

The two corpse statues stood silent. Their eyes scanned the morgue, heads turning in tight, spastic jerks. Gibbs struggled less and less until Quinn could no longer hear him wriggling in the clay.

Randall looked to Martin, who nodded, and the two of them made their way slowly up the stairs, the floorboards flexing loudly under their weight.

"Is it safe, you think?"

Quinn didn't want to be stuck in there any longer. The metal tub was stifling, the air heavy and stale. Gibbs was still in trouble. Judging by the way Randall and Martin moved, he guessed they were pretty slow. They had time.

He opened the lid, limbs finally free of aches and cramps. The cool embalming room air felt good, but the smell was even stronger, now.

Wendy knelt beside Gibbs. He was barely visible beneath the mountain of wet clay. A leather loafer poked out of the mess.

"Quick!" Wendy said. "We gotta get him out."

Quinn searched around until he found tools that looked

disturbingly similar to ice cream scoopers. Trying not to think of what those actually scooped, he gave one to Wendy and they hurriedly dug out the mortician.

Wendy pressed her head against his chest.

"He's in shock." She shook her head as if trying to get rid of a bad thought. "As much as I am." She got up and slicked clay off her arms.

"We need to go," Quinn said. He looked at the clock. They'd been stuck in the morgue for more than an hour. The Town Hall meeting had been over for a while. People would start wondering where they were.

"We can't just leave him," Wendy protested.

"He's breathing," Quinn said. "He'll be okay. We'll have Hector go straight home and tell his mom."

"And what am I supposed to tell my Dad?"

Quinn rubbed the back of his neck. "I don't know. The truth? But that might not do any good. I'll do the same."

Wendy pointed to Gibbs. "He'll believe now. He has to."

"I hope so."

A loud bang from upstairs sent them both jumping.

"Dad?"

Abbie!

"What do we do?" Wendy whispered.

"Ah!"

The loud cry ended abruptly, followed by a loud thump.

Quinn raced up the stairs. Terror had made his legs numb beneath him and as he entered the parlor lobby, he found Abbie passed out on the floor. Beside her, two lines of wet clay led down the carpet and out the side door like the trail of giant slugs.

He knelt down and pressed his ear to Abbie's chest, listening for a heartbeat.

"Is she okay?"

Wendy's voice startled Quinn so bad he felt like he'd jump out of his own skin.

"She's okay," he said. "But I don't think she will be when she wakes up."

"We need to go."

Quinn looked down at Abbie, her face strangely peaceful. But he knew it would only be a short while before she woke up. And then the nightmares would begin.

"Alright," he said. He placed his hand on top of Abbie's. "It'll be okay," he told her, hoping that she could hear him. "We're sending help."

They found Hector stuffed inside a garbage can. He tried to climb out, but ended up tipping over and spilling out into the alleyway.

"Jeeze!" he cried. "Didn't you guys hear me? What the heck was going on in there? I gave the signal!"

"We heard," Wendy said. "But we didn't have time."

"They woke up," Quinn said. "Both of them."

Hector's mouth hung open in shock.

"And where are they?"

"Gone."

His eyes widened. "What? We have to go! Tell everyone! Get the pitchforks and torches!"

"No," Quinn said. "We need you to get your mom. Gibbs is in there and he needs help."

"My mom? But she thinks we're still at my place."

"Abbie and her dad need medical help, so you're gonna have to tell her anyway," Wendy said.

Hector threw up his hands. "She's gonna skin me alive!" He paused. "Well, maybe not, if I tell on Maria first."

"We're all in the same boat," Quinn said. "But we have to do it. Bite the bullet. Take our punishments. And once this is all over, they'll thank us."

Hector scoffed. "Yeah, sure. If those things don't turn the whole town into a wax museum."

They gathered their bikes and rode out.

"Did you see how strong they were?" Wendy asked.

"Yeah," Quinn said. "Now we know what knocked Randall's door down. What smashed Martin's car."

"Wait," Hector said, slowing. "No we don't."

Quinn and Wendy stopped beside him.

"Guys, there must be an original one out there somewhere. It had to *turn* Randall and Martin into those things. Like they tried to turn Gibbs."

"Like Dracula," Quinn said.

"Like Dracula," Hector echoed. "But instead of fangs, it's…you know…clay puke."

Wendy made a sour face.

"The original," Quinn said. "You think that's what grabbed me in the cave?"

"I'd bet my entire comic stash on it. My Atari, too."

"And what about the rabbi?" Wendy asked. "That whole thing was just as weird."

Rabbi Shwartz had told Gibbs he was working with Henry. Quinn knew that wasn't true.

Why would he lie to the undertaker?

And what had he been looking for on those bodies?

"If anyone knows where the original is, it must be him," Quinn said.

"Bet your stash on it?" Hector asked.

"The whole thing."

The Crypt Crew split up, pedaling their separate ways.

Quinn pumped his legs as fast as he could, racing down the empty streets towards Henry and home.

"You'll have to believe me, now," he said to himself.

If not, we're all doomed.

Unwelcome Company

"Henry!" Quinn burst through the front door and into the den.

"Henry, you have to come see. There was this whole—"

He stopped in the doorway.

Henry was sitting on the couch, cup of coffee in hand. Across from him was Rabbi Shwartz. Both of them looked up at Quinn, who wavered, now totally unsure of what to say.

He's here. The thought screamed inside his brain, loud as a siren.

In my house.

The monster.

Or the monster's maker.

Seeing the rabbi sipping coffee in the living room was surreal.

His stomach turned to ice when he saw what was on the center of the coffee table. A muddy boot. The one he'd lost at the Falls.

"Come sit down, Q," Henry said.

Quinn did as instructed, goose bumps forming on his arms as he sat down on the loveseat. Both Henry and the rabbi were studying him, and he felt his cheeks burning. He shifted awkwardly in the chair.

"What's he doing here?" he asked, nodding to the rabbi.

Henry bristled. "Excuse me? Show a little respect, Quinn. The rabbi—"

"But—"

"And speaking of respect," he leaned forward and picked up the mud-caked boot. Quinn could clearly see his initials marked in blocky ink on the label. "Rabbi Shwartz said he found this up at the Falls." Henry's eyes narrowed, and Quinn recoiled. "After three kids came running out of the caves." He set the boot down. "You have some explaining to do, pal. Big time."

Quinn glanced at the rabbi, who sat with his coffee steaming in his hand, examining Quinn with a cool gaze.

"We...we were looking for clues. About the Snatcher. We were trying to help, and we—"

"*This* isn't the kind of help I need," Henry snapped. "It's bad enough my friends are gone. The last thing, the very last thing I need is for you to go sneaking out after midnight for some cave crawling with your friends, pretending to play detective."

Henry's words stabbed Quinn like a dagger through his heart.

"This isn't pretend. This isn't one of your comic book stories. What if you got hurt? What if something happened to Hector or Wendy? Did anyone know where you were? How long do you think it would take for someone to find you if something happened? What if—" he stopped himself, teeth grinding.

Quinn knew what Henry was about to say.

What if I lost you, just like I lost them?

"I'm sorry," Quinn said. "But honest, Henry, there's something—" he paused, looking at the rabbi, unsure of how much he could say in the man's presence. He shut his mouth.

"Don't be too harsh on him," the rabbi said, speaking for the first time. "Please. I didn't mean to cause trouble."

Oh, yeah? Quinn thought. *Then why would you bring my boot? Where were you during the fireworks? When the whole town was out on the green?*

"I only came because I'm worried about you. Both of you."

Sure, Quinn thought with a sneer.

"Rabbi Shwartz has been helping me through all this," Henry said.

"And I'm glad to do it." He turned to Quinn. "In light of all this... unpleasantness, your brother has decided to embrace his faith."

"It's helped, Q. It really has. I told him about the nightmares...about the river. The rabbi is a wise man."

"That's...that's great," Quinn said, trying his best to sound encouraging.

"It's wonderful," the rabbi said. "We have so few Jewish members of the community. It's nice to have an old face back in the fold."

So now Henry will be in your clutches. Nice and close, where you can see him, Quinn thought darkly.

"We've been talking about you coming back, too, Quinn," the rabbi continued. "It's never too late to start preparing for your bar mitzvah."

"But Henry," Quinn said, no longer able to hold back, "the monsters—"

Henry slammed a hand on the table. "Quinn, *enough* with that!"

"But they're real, and I think—"

The rabbi rose from the couch. "I'm sorry, boys. I can see you both have a lot to discuss."

Henry rubbed his face. "Sure. Sorry, rabbi."

"No need to apologize. I can only imagine how hard this has been on you. And know that my door is always open."

"Quinn, get the rabbi's coat and see him out. You'll have to come by for another coffee soon. I could use the company. And the advice."

The rabbi nodded and followed Quinn to the entryway.

Quinn shoved the pea coat into the rabbi's hands, avoiding eye contact.

"You know," the rabbi said softly, "I *do* know a thing or two about monsters."

Quinn looked up, startled.

"You..." He was at a loss for words.

"Monsters come in all shapes and sizes," the rabbi said. "Both human and...other. And let me tell you something, Quinn: they're equally dangerous. We must be vigilant in the presence of monsters. We must fight them, however we can, for as long as we can. I hope to see you at the synagogue. But if you choose not to come, I won't be upset. Shalom."

He donned his coat and let himself out into the night.

Quinn waited at the door, watching as the rabbi disappeared into the darkness, turning the words over in his mind.

Monsters.

Human.

And *Other*.

"What are you up to, rabbi?" he whispered into the night breeze.

Only the soft rustle of leaves and chirp of tree frogs answered.

Quinn shut the door, making sure to check the deadbolt twice.

When he went back to the living room, Henry was coming out of the hallway carrying something wrapped in plastic. He set it down on the couch, and Quinn saw that it was his best suit, neatly pressed and cleaned.

"Getting ready for the funerals," he said. "I need to reach out to Brent, but I don't think he has a phone in the cabin. He should be there, too."

"About the funerals," Quinn said. "Henry, there's something going on. Something that you really need to understand."

"I'm trying, Q. I really am. But if this is another story about monsters, or shadows and rocks coming to life, I really can't right now. Half the town wants me out. The meeting tonight just about confirmed that. They want answers. Not ghost stories. If I can't catch this Snatcher soon, I'm out of a job."

"There won't *be* any funerals," Quinn said forcefully.

Henry paused. "What do you mean?"

"They're not dead," Quinn said. "That's what I've been trying to tell you. Randall and Martin are *alive*. Well, not alive. They've *changed*. Mr. Link, too. It's all—"

"Because of the clay? Q, I know it was a gruesome sight, but they're still human underneath. Believe me, I'll be having nightmares about that. I'm sorry you had to see it."

"That's not what I'm talking about!" Quinn cried. "Henry, they're not dead! They got up and *moved*!"

Henry's eyes narrowed. "And how would you know that?"

Quinn's face paled.

"Please," Henry said, "*Please* tell me you did not seriously break into the funeral home. Quinn, I swear, if you—"

"They almost killed Mr. Gibbs! And Abbie!"

It was Henry's turn to pale.

"They got up," Quinn said. "And tried to...tried to turn Gibbs into one of them."

Henry didn't say anything as he stomped down the hallway into his room. Quinn heard the door slam shut, and suddenly found himself afraid to be alone in the den. He moved to the windows, looking out into the moonlit woods surrounding the house. A branch snapped loudly in the dark. Quinn crouched at the window, slowly moving towards the lamp against the wall. He pulled on the chain, allowing his eyes to adjust to the dark, and peeked through the glass.

Two figures were moving through the woods. Branches and bushes rustled in their wake.

"Henry!"

His brother emerged, fully dressed in his deputy uniform. Quinn glanced down at his belt, noting the always empty gun holster. He wished Henry carried one now, instead of his trusty wooden baton.

"What?" He asked. "And it better be quick, because I'm going to Gibbs' place right now. And the newspaper office. If someone attacked them, they could still be in the area. And you are to *stay here*. I can't keep an eye on you while I go check this out."

Quinn pointed to the window.

"Henry..."

"I mean it, Q. I've never had to pull the big brother card, but I'm pulling it now. You're grounded. If I wanted, I could arrest you. Do you understand how serious this is?"

"Henry!"

"What?"

"You don't have to go to the funeral home," he said, his voice cracking.

Henry cocked his head. "Huh?"

A clay-covered fist smashed through the window. Shards of glass exploded into the den. Henry grabbed a hold of Quinn's shoulder and dragged him down.

Randall's face appeared in the broken window. With a loud grunt, he forced his way into the house.

"Randall?" Henry said, picking himself up. He held out his hands. "Randall? Can you hear me, buddy? It's Henry. I'm not going to hurt you."

Randall studied him with yellow eyes. In a terrifyingly swift motion, he picked up the loveseat with one hand and heaved it across the room. Henry ducked just in time as the sofa crashed into the wall. A family portrait fell and shattered to pieces.

"Randall!" Henry cried. "It's me! What are you doing?"

The clay monstrosity sprang forward. Henry sidestepped his lunge, grabbing an iron poker from the fireplace.

He wielded it in front of him like a sword.

"I mean it, Randall. I don't want to hurt you. I just want to know what's going on. But if you don't stop I'll have to—"

A pair of arms wrapped around Henry's chest, yanking him backwards into the kitchen. Quinn scrambled behind the couch.

Martin was holding Henry in a tight grip. Randall made pounding motions with his fist against a palm.

Quick, Quinn thought. *You have to distract them*!

"Hey!" he cried.

Randall turned with a loud crunching sound like stone scraping stone.

Quinn grabbed a paperweight from the coffee table, aimed, and threw as hard as he could. The metal globe made a loud crunching sound as it slammed into Randall's face, chipping off a few chunks of clay.

He ignored Quinn as if he were an annoying fly.

Henry kicked up his feet, sending Martin tumbling back. They both fell onto the kitchen table, splitting the oak in two. In the fall, Henry was able to free himself. He dove for the fire poker, narrowly missing a powerful swing from Randall's fist. Henry rolled away as Randall's blow made a crater in the hardwood floor.

"Quinn! Get on the phone! Call the station!"

Henry made a vicious swing, connecting with Randall's shoulder. Randall stumbled back, huge chunks of clay falling to the floor. He swung again and caught Randall's leg. Randall collapsed against the wall, pots and pans clattering down around him.

Quinn raced back to the den and grabbed the phone. His hands were shaking so badly, he could barely use the rotary.

He put the receiver to his ear.

Silence.

Now the phones were down?

"Quinn!"

Henry and Martin burst through the wall of the kitchen and into the den, wood, and plaster, and sheetrock tumbled across the floor. In the wreckage, Henry struggled beneath Martin. Quinn could see his mouth beginning to open, unhinging like a snake. He knew what would happen next.

He grabbed a shovel from the fireplace. Not as good a weapon as the poker, but it would have to do.

"YOU!" he screamed. "GET AWAY FROM MY BROTHER!"

Martin looked up, his mouth opening wider and wider. Slimy clay dripped from his lips.

Quinn swung the shovel with everything he had. It cracked against Martin's face, exposing a good piece of his chin beneath the clay. Henry kicked his way out from underneath the pile of wood and sheetrock, covered in cuts.

They clutched onto one another.

"Quinn, I'm sorry."

"You just had to see for yourself."

"Yeah." Henry wiped a smear of blood from his nose. "Guess I did."

Martin remained crumpled on the floor. Quinn saw Randall in the kitchen, trying to stand up on his shattered leg.

"What could have done this?" Henry asked. "How are they still alive?"

A loud crack echoed from the front of the house.

The brothers, armed with the poker and the shovel, crept to the foyer. The front door was splintered, laying in pieces ten feet into the house.

The thing that stood there, silhouetted in the porch light, turned Quinn's guts to jelly.

It was a child, or what a child would look like if it were molded from clay. It had no eyes, only black holes where eyes should have been. It stood a little shorter than Quinn, but that's where all comparisons ended. Its arms were long. Too long. They drooped like thin noodles, and the hands that were attached weren't hands at all, but long claws, like a lobster without the pincer. They dragged on the ground behind it, the noodle like arms moving like tentacles. Its legs were short, but the feet were the biggest Quinn had ever seen. Each foot was at least three feet long. There were no toes, just giant pieces of clay that ended in sharp points.

Snowshoes, he thought.

Everyone thought they were snowshoes.

Instead of walking on its enormous feet, it pulled itself along bit by bit with those tentacle-like arms, the points of the claws digging into the ground, scraping up the hardwood as it heaved itself forward.

Quinn could make out something written on its forehead. Carved in, more like, as if by a hammer and chisel. But he couldn't make out the word. He was too busy backing away and clutching onto Henry to make much sense of anything.

The creature came closer, pulling itself along much quicker than Quinn expected it could. The mouth opened. It made a sound like an insect chirping. Its black eyes fell on Henry, and the sound turned from a chirp into a chitter, like one of those joke dentures at Malman's shop. The ones that wound up and chomped all on their own.

"Quinn, I want you to stay behind me. If anything happens, you run down the street and get help."

Quinn tried to answer, but his voice failed him.

Henry charged forward, iron poker raised high. Before he could swing, the creature's arms shot out with lightning speed and slashed him. Henry went crashing back to the floor. The creature didn't slow. It grabbed him in its claws, pulling him in, closer and closer. Its mouth opened. The teeth chomped and gnashed hungrily.

The Deputy badge snapped from Henry's chest, sending the metal skidding across the floor, landing at Quinn's feet.

"Stop!" Quinn said.

The creature looked at Quinn with dead, black eyes.

Quinn reached down and snatched up the badge.

"Don't hurt him," he said. "If you want someone, take me!"

The creature didn't let go of Henry. Quinn watched his brother try to free himself, but the claws tightened around him, pinning him to the floor.

"Leave him alone!" Quinn said, and readied his shovel.

He gripped the handle, preparing for an all-or-nothing attack that would either save Henry or doom them both.

"That's my brother," Quinn said through gritted teeth. "And no one messes with my brother."

Two powerful hands grabbed him, squeezing so hard Quinn was afraid his arms would break. The shovel slipped from his hands. Randall had him on one side, Martin on the other.

"Quinn!" Henry gasped. The creatures gripped tighter and he cried out in pain.

"Stop it!" Quinn screamed, his throat raw. "Stop it!"

But they didn't stop. They held him still as the creature opened its mouth.

"No!"

The swamp-stink filled the room as mud and clay poured forth, drenching Henry until he was lost underneath a bubbling, steaming pile. Quinn struggled against the stony strength of his captors, stomping on their feet, kicking their shins, which hurt him more than anything.

He watched helplessly as the clay hardened around Henry like a foul-smelling cocoon. Henry struggled at first, but as the creature spat out more and more of the stuff, he went still.

Quinn could hardly see through the tears streaming down his face. He could no longer feel his arms or legs. Only a cold numbness that seemed to wrap itself around his entire body.

The creature closed its mouth and cocked its head, studying Henry. With its long, skinny arms, it began to wrap him up, almost like a carpet, and turned away, dragging him out into the night.

It disappeared into the darkness, leaving behind a trail of wet clay.

He felt Randall and Martin's hands grip the sides of his neck. His vision began to fade. Quinn could hear a thumping sound in the dark. Maybe it was his heart. The sound swelled, beating hard and wild as war drums.

Quinn's world went black.

A Town in Terror

Quinn swam in the darkness, drifting from one nightmare to the next. Haunting visions flooded his mind. Henry screaming in the arms of the creature. Faces of clay melting to puddles of blood. Shadows reaching, wrapping their claws around his neck. They went on and on, relentless, until a soft light penetrated all that blackness.

Somewhere up above, a voice floated through the din.

"Hey. Hey, Q. You awake?"

Quinn's eyes fluttered open, and he found himself in the searing light of day.

Hector was standing over him, sweaty and out of breath.

"Oh, thank God."

"Where am I?"

"You don't recognize your best buddy's room?"

Quinn sat up painfully, pushing himself back until he was up against the headboard. He looked around, noticing all the *Critters*, *Star Wars*, and lucha libre posters adorning the walls.

"How..."

"How'd you get here?"

Quinn nodded. Winced. His neck was still killing him.

"Rabbi Shwartz found you," he said. "He brought you to the clinic, and mom brought you here."

"Henry..." Quinn found it difficult to speak, like something in his throat had been crushed.

Hector's face dropped.

"Don't know, Q. No sign of him. Mom tried calling the station, but all the lines are dead."

"No," he said. "I...I saw..." He put his head back on the pillow, a sharp pain stabbing behind his eyes.

"What do you remember?"

Quinn stared at the ceiling. In a soft voice, he told Hector what had happened.

"And they just took him," he said. "Out into the dark."

Heavy silence hung in the room.

Quinn felt something cool and metal in his pocket. Henry's badge. He held it close, warming it with his hands.

I'll hold onto this for you, he thought. *Until you come back*.

"We'll find him," Hector finally said. "Mom's been talking with a few of the men from town. They're forming a search party."

"Who?" Quinn asked.

"Mr. Arpin, for one. It was his idea. And Wendy's dad. Mr. Castelot also volunteered. The town needs to vote in a new Deputy." He paused, wincing. "Just to fill in, until they find Henry."

"And who's that?"

"Don't know," Hector said. "But right now, there's a curfew. No one out after sundown. And Mr. Castelot's group will be patrolling from sunset to sunrise. A few others, too. The ones who still have gas for their trucks. It's the best they can do, until the bridge crew starts work and the State Police can get here."

"I can help," Quinn said. He sat up, head spinning. "I can show them where—"

"It's alright," Hector said, putting a hand on Quinn's chest. "Mr. Francis and Mr. Arpin checked out your house. They already started following the trail."

But they don't know what they're dealing with, Quinn thought. *None of them do.*

"Mr. Arpin is a big-time hunter and trapper," Hector said reassuringly. "He knows the woods like the back of his hand. So don't you worry. Mom says you're lucky. Made it out with a couple of scratches, and that's about it."

"Good," Quinn said. Still, he felt like he'd been run over by a steamroller.

Hector went to his dresser and grabbed an envelope. "The rabbi left this for you. Told me to give to you as soon as you woke up."

Hector hopped onto the bed, peering over Quinn's shoulder as he opened the letter.

> Quinn,
> I think I might have an idea as to the nature of this monster. Come to Beth Shalom as soon as you can. And bring that Delgado boy and the Francis girl, too.
> Hope you are ready to hear what I have to say.
> Ephraim Shwartz

"Yikes," Hector said. "You sure you want to go? That's like walking right into Dracula's lair." He was trying to joke, but Quinn could hear the waver in his voice.

Quinn reread the letter.

"I don't think so," he said. "I think we were wrong about the rabbi." He got up from the bed, stretching his limbs. "Right now, it's the best chance we have. I say we take it."

Hector shook his head. "I don't like this, Q. I don't think Wendy will, either."

The rabbi knows something, Quinn thought. *Whether he's behind all this or not, he knows something.*

"We have to at least try," Quinn said. "Henry is still out there. And he won't be the last."

Hector's face dropped.

"What is it?"

"Maria," he said. "Mom went to wake her this morning and found her window open. She's out looking right now with Terry and Frank's folks."

"You think they're taking the logging trail?"

Hector nodded.

"I'm sorry, Hector."

"Me too. I told her it was a stupid idea. But she went anyway. The Scouts are her whole life. She..." He turned away. "You know how many times I wished she would just...just *disappear*? I even asked my abuela if there was some kind of spell I could use." He turned back, his eyes red and watery. "I wish there were a spell to bring her back, now. Never thought I'd miss her. You know?"

"We'll go to the synagogue. Talk to the rabbi. We'll find Henry and Maria. I promise. But we're stopping by my place, first."

"What for?"

"Firepower, of course."

Hector swallowed hard. "Of course."

"Just a precaution," Quinn said. "I'd feel a whole lot better knowing we had some kind of defense." He shrugged. "And a pocketful of fireworks would sure make me feel a heck of a lot safer. I've seen what these things can do."

"I don't know how keen I am on monster hunting, Q. I couldn't even stand up to my own sister. I've messed up so many times, and I—"

"Don't talk like that," Quinn said. "You're brave, Hector. I need you with me. No one takes our families away. *No one*."

It was an overcast day and the gray sky, bloated with dark clouds, seemed to reflect the state of the town below.

Main Street was near deserted. Quinn and Hector rode by signs plastered to streetlights.

CURFEW: SEVEN O'CLOCK
   NO ONE OUT AFTER SUNDOWN
   STAY INSIDE. LOCK YOUR DOORS

A huge assortment of flowers and signs stood where Randall and Martin's bodies had been discovered. The bandstand was covered in wreaths and small flags. It looked like a gravesite.

Along the benches and storefront windows were signs reading:

PROTECT THE CHILDREN OF STARK FALLS

MISSING: TERRY POTS
    FRANK CASTELOT
    MARIA DELGADO

LAST SEEN ON MAIN STREET, FIVE O'CLOCK WEDNESDAY NIGHT

IF FOUND, ESCORT TO STARK COUNTY SHERIFF'S OFFICE

BRING OUR KIDS HOME SAFE

And a final sign scrawled hastily in black paint read:

BEWARE THE SNOWSHOE SNATCHER

"Boys!"

They slowed outside Malman and Son's. Mr. Malman was in the doorway, beckoning them.

The store was empty. It was unusual, especially on a Saturday afternoon. Mr. Malman clapped Quinn on the shoulder, his face drawn. White stubble covered his cheeks and chin. Quinn had never seen him without a clean shave.

"I'm so sorry, Quinn. I know how it is to lose someone you love." He looked at the framed photo of Ethan. "And you too, Hector. I know how close you were with your sister."

"They're not dead," Hector said emphatically. "Just missing."

Malman nodded slowly. "Yes. Yes, of course. We'll find them, soon enough. In the meantime, I wanted to tell you that if you need anything, anything at all, don't hesitate to ask. You're my children, you know. I've told you that many times, but I mean it."

"Thanks, Mr. Malman," Quinn said. "Really. But we have to get going."

Malman's brows rose. "Where are you off to in such a hurry?"

"Investigating," Hector answered. "Following up on some leads."

Malman frowned. "Sounding like a sheriff there, Hector."

"It's true," Quinn said. "But it's best you don't know about it. No offense, Mr. Malman. We just...want to keep this a secret, if we can."

"Secrets, secrets," Malman said. "Well, yours is safe with me."

"Has there been any word? Anything about the search for Maria and them?"

Malman shook his head. "Sadly, no. Mr. Castelot and Mrs. Pots were in here about an hour ago." He pointed to two framed pictures of the boys standing on the register. "They asked to leave these here. As if I don't know those faces. Chased them out of here more times than I can count."

Hector and Quinn shared an uncomfortable glance.

"But I *do* hope they turn up safe and sound. Before you go, I have something for you." He went and rummaged behind the counter, emerging with a small package wrapped in brown paper.

"It finally came in," he said, placing it into Quinn's hands.

Quinn undid the twine and unwrapped it. It was a copy of Stephen King's latest book, *It*.

"But, this isn't supposed to be out until September," Quin said, staring at the cover.

"Well, I have my ways. Open it,"

Quinn flipped to the first page.

To Quinn,
This is for all your help this past year. I hope you treasure it forever.
With love,
Jonas

Quinn smiled. It felt so strange, seeing Mr. Malman's first name like that. He'd found that adult's first names were like secrets, secrets kids were never meant to find out. Mr. Malman had made it a point to share his.

"This is...this is just awesome, Mr. Malman. Honest. Thank you!"

Mr. Malman opened his arms, and Quinn leaned in to give him a hug. It felt good.

"It's the least I can do," he said softly. "Things will get better, Quinn. Believe me."

Quinn stepped back. Tears glistened behind Malman's coke bottle lenses.

"Well," the old man said. "Far be it from me to impede your investigation, boys. Go forth and solve crime." He paused. "That reminds me, did either of you boys get the *Minuteman* delivered today?"

When they told him no, the old man's face creased in a fine web of wrinkles. "Strange. That Mr. Harwich is a hindrance, mark my words. But it feels strange not starting the morning with one of his ridiculous write-ups."

I'd tell you, Quinn thought. But what good would it do? We need to solve this, and fast.

As they left Malman and Son's, Quinn packed the book into the basket on his bike, nestling it beside the cherry bombs, m-80's, Roman candles, and Mr. Link's mythology text.

A truck circled the green. It looped around to slow beside them. Jacques Arpin leaned out the driver's side window.

"You boys alright?"

"Holding up," Quinn managed.

"Uh huh," Mr. Arpin said. "Just be careful. And stay on the main roads. He sighed, peering up at the surrounding mountains. "Those poor kids. They're out there, somewhere. We'll find them. Your brother, too."

Quinn saw a rifle in the passenger seat, and his stomach knotted.

"Mr. Francis is patrolling the other side of town. Wherever you boys are headed, make sure you get there and back by sundown. Whatever's out there seems to do its dirty work under the moonlight."

"We will, Mr. Arpin."

"You know, back in Quebec, we had this legend, the Loup-Garou. Something akin to a werewolf. Stalked people in the night. Changed back to a man in the morning. I used to love my grandma's stories about the Loup-Garou." His grin faded. "Not anymore. This town's got a case of the willies, and I guess I caught it bad. Be safe, boys."

The truck's engine rattled as he pulled away, disappearing down Hodges Road.

"So…you sure about this? The rabbi?"

Quinn clutched Henry's badge like a talisman. A light drizzle of rain began to fall. Far off in the distance, a low rumble of thunder shook the sky like the call of some distant monster.

"I'm sure," he said.

Wendy met up with them halfway, since her house was closest to the synagogue. She lived on Miller's End, a small dirt road with little pillbox houses, what the kids of Stark Falls liked to call "The Dredges". It was the last neighborhood in Stark Falls proper, about as close to the edge of town as you could get. And still, the synagogue was even further.

"Dad's been out all night," she told them. "He even got some of his buddies from the mill and the lumberyard together. About twenty of them. They're moving the search up north, past the Falls."

"Good," Quinn said. Henry trusted Dale Francis, and Quinn wouldn't be surprised if he were elected sheriff one day.

"And as for us," she said. "What's the plan?"

"We need to meet with Rabbi Shwartz. Find out what he knows."

Wendy frowned.

"What?"

"Yesterday someone told me one of his windows got smashed in. A brick."

"What? Why?"

"Because of the talk. Rumors, you know? Some people think he's behind it."

"Sound familiar?" Hector asked.

"It was us," Quinn said. Shame filled him, making him feel about two inches tall. "We were the ones talking about him."

"Terry and Hank heard," Wendy said.

"And my sister," Hector said sadly.

Quinn gripped tight onto the handles of his bike.

We made him a monster, he thought bitterly. *We gave everyone the ammo they needed.*

But there was still time.

"This place is going crazy," she said. "You can feel it, real as anything. People are looking for someone to blame. Anyone." She shivered, pulling up the hood of her raincoat.

The Crypt Crew pedaled through the rain, until they reached a narrow gravel drive, and a small building nestled against encroaching forest. Tall grass and tendrils of ivy crept over its sides, covering the soot-stained windows. Its gray bricks and crumbling chimney made it look like some abandoned witches' keep.

They rode up, parking their bikes.

Quinn looked up at the synagogue. The one he'd feared for so long, for reasons he could never quite understand.

As they approached the door, a thunderous cry rose from the side of the building.

"Stop! Stop right there! This is private property, and I'll—"

Rabbi Shwartz rounded the corner, his hair wild, face a mask of fury. He brandished a paint roller in his hand. Quinn staggered back and tripped, his butt landing in a puddle.

"Oh, kids!"

The rabbi pulled Quinn up. "I'm sorry I startled you. I thought you were someone else." He picked up the paint roller. "Come around back."

They followed him. On the wall, large swaths of fresh gray paint were slicked on, but Quinn could still make out the words scrawled in bright red:

JEWS GET OUT

The words screamed from the paint, dripping with hatred.

"Had some unwelcome visitors last night," he said. "I thought they'd returned."

The rabbi dunked the roller into the paint and finished covering it up.

"It happens more often than you'd think. A sad state of affairs in the land of the free and home of the brave. People change, I've found. But not the scared, or the ignorant. And when I see *children* doing it, well...I fear for the future."

The Crypt Crew stood motionless, watching as the rabbi tiredly cast the roller aside, large shoulders slumping.

"I'm glad you came. We have much to discuss."

They followed him into the old stone building. Henry had told Quinn that the synagogue used to be the old one room schoolhouse, back in the old days. Rabbi Shwartz had remodeled it a bit, and though it was tiny, it served the small community of Jewish folks in the county.

Inside, the rabbi led them through a narrow corridor that ended in a staircase.

Hector paused at the top, turning back to Quinn and Wendy with a nervous twitch.

The rabbi was already moving down the stairs and into the cellar.

"Come along!" he called up.

"You first," Hector said, stepping aside to allow Quinn to follow.

"Chicken," Wendy chided.

Quinn walked down the stone stairs, ducking to avoid the thick cobwebs hanging from the ceiling. He'd never been in the basement before and wondered if this really was a mistake. A small synagogue at the edge of the woods seemed as good a place as any to get attacked by a monster.

He took a deep breath, clutching the badge.

You can do this, he told himself.

The basement was much larger than Quinn thought. The cavernous room was lit by a series of gas and oil lamps. Antique wooden furniture lay scattered about, bookshelves covering the walls from top to bottom. It smelled like old books and oil, like some sort of ancient library. A massive oak table sat in the center, and a small wood burning stove radiated a welcoming warmth into the stone cellar.

The rabbi moved to the table, pulling up four chairs. Quinn stood at it, gazing at the array of papers scattered across the surface. There were pages upon pages of hand scribbled notes, along with maps of Stark Falls and the surrounding towns, as well as blueprints for some of the buildings, including the library, town hall, and the textile mill. Another map lay beside it, depicting a series of winding tubes, crisscrossing in mad patterns. He looked at the top of the map, where the rabbi had written *"STARK FALLS SEWER SYSTEM"*.

The rabbi set down a pot of steaming coffee and poured himself a cup. "Please, sit."

The Crypt Crew did so, each shifting a bit uneasily as they gazed around the lantern-lit room.

"It seems," the rabbi said, "that we all have something in common." He paused, looking at each of them with that steely gaze.

"What...what would that be?" Hector asked.

"We have all seen what's infested our town. The evil that preys at night. And I think, like me, you are hunters." He gestured around the table. "So, I wanted to meet with you, as a fellow hunter, and see if we can come up with a plan of action. If not, the thing we hunt may pick off the entire town, one by one, until no one is left. Not *human*, anyway."

"We need to know *what* we're hunting," Wendy said. "My dad's out there. If it's something I can beat, I wanna beat it."

"*Do* you know?" Quinn asked him. "You told me you knew about monsters."

"I do," the rabbi said. "I've known something was amiss ever since the night you found Randall Colburn's house ransacked. I had my suspicions, and so I decided to do some investigating." He pointed to the map. "It turns out, my suspicions were right. The thing that took Randall, Martin, and your brother, the thing that lurks in caves and dark alleys, is a monster I've known all my life."

He leaned forward.

"What we're dealing with, my fellow hunters, is a golem."

The Rabbi's Tale

"Golem?" Hector sounded out the word slowly.

"They're a Jewish legend," Quinn said. "A myth. I haven't heard about them since I was little."

The rabbi's bushy eyebrows raised. "Ah, yes. A myth." He took a long sip of his coffee, steam rising around his tangled beard. "The golem," the rabbi said, "is a creature made from the Earth. Either by clay, or mud, or stone. Certain rabbis would make them, and using the secret name of God, would bring them to life. They are mindless. Obedient, like robots. Over the centuries, they've been used as many things: servants, builders, watchmen, and even warriors, in times of need. It is said that Adam was the original golem, containing the entire universe within his being."

"They sound neat," Hector said. He looked around the table, and, not seeing anyone sharing the sentiment, slid a bit further down on his chair.

"I'm going to tell you a story," the rabbi said. "One that I've not told a soul in sixty-seven years. One that I hope I'll never have to tell again."

The Crypt Crew leaned in, listening intently as the rabbi began his tale.

"I was born and raised in a small village in the Black Forest. It was a tiny place, a settlement of Jewish farmers and metal workers." He grunted. "You won't find it on any map. It's nothing but ruins, now, swallowed up by the woods. And for that, I'm thankful. The rabbi at that time was Jeduda Gotzner. He was a...peculiar man. A student of the Kabbalah."

"What's that?" Wendy asked.

"It's a Jewish tradition," Quinn explained, "one that focuses on mysticism."

"Like magic?" Hector asked.

"I guess so," Quinn supposed, shrugging.

Across the table, the rabbi smiled. "So you haven't forgotten *all* of your education, it seems. Yes, children, I guess you could call it magic. Ancient wisdom. Secret, and very difficult to master. Rabbi Gotzner was the leader, you could say, of our little village. My parents were farmers, but they had higher hopes for me, and so I was chosen to study under him. I didn't want to. Not at first. I was being trained as a metal worker. Believe it or not, there were still blacksmiths in those days. Horses needed shoeing. Tools needed fixing. I was content to swing a hammer and work the forge with old Elkan Weiss, who we children called 'The Bull'.

"I was large, and some thought me clumsy or simple, but Gotzner saw otherwise. He took me under his wing, and soon I was spending more time at the temple than I was at home.

"Gotzner had amassed an enormous library, all sacred rabbinic texts passed down from one generation to the next. Some were very, very old, and from places as far away as Egypt. It was in Rabbi Gotzner's home that my love of reading took hold. I poured through those tomes, unlocking one secret after the next, secrets even the Torah had not shown me in all my years of study.

"Rabbi Gotzner was a serious man. Very serious. And his thirst for hidden knowledge drove him to make long journeys up and down the Rhine, even to Spain and Russia, in order to meet and speak with other Kabbalists. He would leave for months at a time, usually during the winter, and return in the spring with books, scrolls, and manuscripts. I would help him in his research, translating or transcribing, making charts and notes. It was some time before I discovered what the rabbi was *truly* after. He told me that he wanted to try his hand at creating a golem. At first, I laughed. But the look he gave me—the hard, cold determination in his eyes, stopped my laughter dead.

"The rabbi showed me a book I'd never seen before. It was bound in black leather, which I later found out was the skin of an Egyptian crocodile, its pages yellowed and brittle.

"'This,' he told me, 'is my own book, Ephraim. *The Book of Jehuda Gotzner*.'

"I opened it and was stunned to find it littered with illustrations and instructions. Some was in Hebrew, still more in strange pictographs, a sort of hieroglyphic you would find in Egypt or ancient Sumer. I asked where he had learned all of this, and he told me that he'd visited rabbis scattered throughout Europe, pooling knowledge from each, and that he'd separated the truths from the lies. It contained incantations and spells to summon countless shedim. Monsters and demons.

"'If we do this, Ephraim, we will be performing a miracle.'

"And who was I to argue against that? As a Kabbalist scholar in training, one doesn't pass up the chance to witness a miracle, much less create one.

"On the night of June 5th, 1928, I was fourteen years old. That, my fellow hunters, is the night my life would change forever."

The rabbi paused to take a long swig of coffee, and Quinn could see his hands tremble slightly.

"1928?" Hector sounded incredulous. "That was like, a million years ago!"

The rabbi smiled. "Yes, indeed. But this old dinosaur is still here, Mr. Delgado. That first night we gathered clay from the riverbed, and the rabbi ordered me to go to the quarry, where the few stoneworkers we had chipped away rock from the side of the hill. It was hard work that took all day. The rabbi set himself up in old Rudolph Heller's place, a stone tower that used to house grain, but had been converted into a workspace. A laboratory, of a sort. It was nightfall by the time we finished molding the clay, and I, with a hammer and chisel, began to break off great pieces of flint, inserting them into the clay body like bones."

"That's why they're so powerful," Quinn said. "They seem like they're dripping, like you could poke right through them, but they're hard on the inside."

Rabbi Shwartz nodded. "It was always thought that the way to make a golem come to life was to write the Hebrew word for truth, EMETH, somewhere on the body. In the story of the Golem of Prague, the rabbi Judah Loew ben Bezalel did this to awaken his own golem in order to protect the Jews of that city from attack. It worked, or so the stories say. Others say the golem went on a rampage, and it wasn't stopped until the rabbi pulled the shem from its mouth."

"The what?" Hector asked.

"The *shem*," Rabbi Shwartz repeated. "Is the name of God. Or one of the many names. These are written onto a piece of parchment, sealed in a capsule, and inserted into the Golem's mouth. This brings the creature to life."

Hector and Wendy exchanged a wide-eyed look. "That sounds easy. Like, scary easy."

"One would think," he said, "Yet when we did this, our golem did nothing. The clay creature remained dormant. We recited the alphabet from the *Sefer Yetzirah*, circling as we did so, forwards, and then backwards, just as the stories said. I looked to Rabbi Gotzner and asked if we'd made a mistake. He told me we hadn't. It was a test, you see, and a lesson. For the true way to create a golem was something much different, and only Gotzner himself possessed the knowledge.

"'It must be built for a single purpose,' he'd said, 'To till the fields, for example. Or cut down lumber. Or tend to a household as a servant. What we must do, Ephraim, is decide what we want our golem to do, and mark the word here,' he pointed to the chest. 'and write it here,' he pointed to the parchment. 'And not insert it into the mouth, but into the chest, where a man's heart would lie beating.'

"The Rabbi had learned something else in all his travels. Something even the most dedicated rabbinical scholars missed. For a golem to live, to truly live, you cannot use words and shem alone. There is another element."

He paused, his gaze very far away.

"Rabbi?"

"Yes," he said, shaking himself back to the present. "You see, it was a tragedy that gave us what we needed to make the golem. Our village was peaceful, understand, but the surrounding towns were not. Hunters would come from the towns further along the valley and trample through our crops. Sometimes they would steal, or cause trouble in the tavern. When they came, or anyone from the government, we were on edge. Jews were not treated kindly all the time.

"It has been so since our people left the lands of Israel, and so it was in 1928, when a drunken hunter threw a five-year-old child into the village well."

"Oh, no!" Wendy said, covering her mouth.

The Rabbi hung his head.

"The man was out of his mind, and already fighting two villagers at once. The boy had come out to see what all the ruckus was about and got too close. The hunter, in his fury, must have thought he was another man joining in, and so he shoved the boy right over the stone wall. All we could do was watch as he fell down into the cold, wet dark.

"We sat shiva for little Fritz Lessing, and after the village mourned, we buried him in the boneyard. Rabbi Gotzner was furious and didn't leave his tower for many days. I went to see him one night and found him furiously working in the lab, his arms and chest covered in globs of clay. On the table was a golem, though it didn't look like a man. It was far too large. Seven feet tall, at least, with fists the size of war hammers and a head heavy and flat-topped as a battering ram.

"I asked him what he was doing.

"'Working a miracle,' he told me. 'And this one will not fail. Not in the least.'

"He beckoned me closer, and as I drew near, something on the workbench caught my attention. It was a lock of hair. Golden blonde. Fritz' hair.

"'What is this?' I asked, outraged.

"Rage bubbled under the rabbi's words. 'The demon took one of ours,' he spat, 'and now, we shall take him.'

"He placed the hair inside a metal capsule, and along with the shem, inserted it into the golem's chest.

"'To make them wake, we must give them a part of us.'

"I was disgusted. The rabbi had gone to the graveyard, dug up the boy, and clipped a lock of his hair. I called him a necromancer, but he laughed off my anger.

"'You want justice for Fritz, yes? Then help me in my work and pester me no further!'

"It shames me, now, but I helped him finish sculpting the golem. Once we were done, instead of writing TRUTH on the chest, the rabbi took a chisel and carved the word REVENGE."

He wrote the Hebrew characters for the Crew.

נְקָמָה

"The word chilled me to look upon, and as the rabbi inserted the lock of hair and the shem, the golem sat up. I stumbled back. Frightened isn't even close to describing it. I was terrified. And I'll never forget Rabbi Gotzner's laughter. I told him I wanted no part of this, not if it would lead to violence. But he told me I was already in too deep. I had learned the secret, the sacred knowledge, and there would be no going back.

"I stood and watched in horror as the golem climbed down off the bench, stretching to its full height. The rabbi whispered in Hebrew, 'Go, now. And avenge.'

"The giant creature nodded, and without pause, or thought, or a soul, left the tower, its footsteps shaking the ground like tremors.

"I didn't sleep that night, and when I emerged from my house, I found the entire village gathered in the square, pointing in the direction of the forest.

"The golem emerged from the woods, cradling a body in its arms. The hunter who had mistakenly killed little Fritz. The clay monster didn't slow its pace as it passed by the terrified villagers and lurched up into Gotzner's tower.

"The Rabbi emerged cackling, raving. He held up his arms in triumph. The villagers met that day to decide what was to be done. Surely the hunter's friends and family, his whole *town*, would descend on our village with murder in their hearts and steel in their hands. Jews were not loved, and if it ever came to light that a rabbi had created a monster, it would only end in our sorrow.

"We decided to bury the body and speak no more of what we'd seen.

"Days passed, and Rabbi Gotzner never emerged from his tower. Finally, the villagers begged me to investigate. I was the only one brave enough, they said. Or stupid enough, I secretly thought.

"I called for the rabbi at the base of the tower, but heard nothing.

But as I climbed up the winding stairs towards the laboratory, I could hear a great struggle. Choking sounds, muffled screams, and heavy footfalls. I threw open the door and found the golem throttling the rabbi by his neck. The old man dropped to the ground. I ran to him.

"'Stop them,' he told me. 'Ephraim, you have to stop them.'

"'Them?' I asked. 'What them?'

"I was so concerned for the rabbi that I hadn't paid attention to my surroundings. Ten more golems stood along the walls, watching in silence. The rabbi had been busy, building his own monstrous army. Yet these did not have REVENGE carved into their chests, and their eyes burned like hot coals. Each one was marked with the Hebrew word for DESTROY."

Again, he wrote the letters:

הוֹרְסִים

"'What have you done?' I demanded.

"'An army,' he said. 'My army…'

"I looked at the golems' red glowing eyes. And it was then I realized that I had spent my life studying under an evil man.

"'The…book…' the rabbi gurgled. 'Take it…keep it safe. The way to kill…to kill them…is in death. Death, Ephraim. You must…must write…'

"Rabbi Gotzner's eyes rolled up into his head, and he spoke no more.

"I knew what I had to do.

"I raced to the smithy, where I took Elkan Weiss' biggest hammer and a handful of chisels. With a blade, I carved the word METH, or DEATH, onto each. I raced back to the tower, but in my absence, the ten golems marked DESTROY had vanished. Only the original remained."

Rabbi Shwartz held up his hands.

"In my first battle with a golem, I lost three fingers of my right hand. I would lose the ones on the left later. But that first fight was my biggest lesson. My proving ground. To destroy a golem, one must remove the shem from inside of it, or carve the word DEATH into its forehead, so the stories said. Gotzner's book had the *true* way.

"The *only* way to destroy a golem and be sure of it.

"It lunged at me, astonishingly fast for something so blocky and tall and heavy. I rolled out of the way as a bookcase toppled just inches away. When I stood, I readied one of the chisels and gripped the hammer as hard as I could. My vision tunneled. All I could see was the creature's chest. REVENGE. I charged, and with a hard swing, managed to drive the chisel into the Golem like a railroad spike. A loud crack echoed through the lab and set my ears ringing. But the chisel hadn't pierced deep enough. Instead, it snapped, and the golem grabbed me, opened its mouth, and crunched down on my hand with a row of sharpened stone teeth. I didn't even feel it at first. There was no time. I had to destroy it. I shifted the hammer to my left hand, and with my mangled right I set another chisel marked DEATH against the clay demon.

"That time, my aim was true. The hammer *cracked*. The chisel pierced. And the Golem fell, breaking into pieces as chunks of clay toppled onto me like I was trapped under a falling building.

"The next day, we put the tower to the torch. As the village watched Gotzner's evil playground burn, I set off, my hand bandaged, my belt filled with marked chisels, a hammer slung around my back. I bid my farewells and did not return for many, many years.

"I traveled through Europe, hunting down the escaped golems. It took a long time. Decades.

"One, I destroyed in the streets of Madrid. Another in the catacombs beneath Paris. One high in the Swiss Alps, another on the banks of the Black Sea. They fled to Russia, to Holland. One eluded me across the sea, and I caught up with it in Morocco, where it crumbled into the desert sand.

"The last I tracked the longest, and the creature led me to the ends of the Earth. It was in Finnmark, the northernmost part of Norway, in a town called Hammerfest, nestled on the banks of the Arctic Ocean. It's the most northern town in the world. Like standing on the edge of the Earth itself. I always found that odd, that my last battle with the hammer should be in Hammerfest. I'd received word that the townsfolk had spotted a troll."

"Are those real, too?" Hector interrupted.

"Are what real?" Rabbi Shwartz asked.

"Well, you know. *Trolls*. I mean, if there's golems, then..."

"I don't know, Hector," the rabbi said, "but I wouldn't be surprised. Not anymore."

Hector looked to Quinn, mouthing a big 'Woooowwww' as the rabbi continued.

"I'd heard such rumors before, especially in the Nordic countries, but something, a feeling, drew me to investigate. And after nearly twenty years, on the outskirts of that cold Norwegian port city, I slew the last of the golems. That one took even more from me."

The rabbi lifted his leg, slamming it down on the table. The Crew slid back their chairs, startled as he drew up one leg of his pants, exposing a wooden prosthetic with metal joints.

"The final golem took my leg, but the people of Hammerfest took care of me. A woodworker, Hans, made this leg, here."

He rolled the pant leg back down and set his fake leg under the table. "It gave me time to reflect, and to further my studies and note my findings. I rested in that town for three months."

"And after?" Wendy asked. "When it was done, where did you go?" She was leaning on her elbows, enthralled.

"The only place I knew. Home. But when I returned, there was no village left. The war. The World War had emptied it. The buildings were still there, but it was a ghost town. My parents. My friends. My neighbors. All gone. Nothing was left for me. Only memories. And so I traveled north, back to Hammerfest and Hans, who had kept something hidden for me."

"The book," Quinn said. "Gotzner's book!"

"Indeed. He'd done as I asked, and kept it safe. I thanked him, and from that small Norwegian port, booked passage here. To America. Where I thought I would settle in a quiet place, near a forest like my homeland's, and care for a small temple if anyone kept the faith."

He clapped his hands.

"And so, my fellow hunters, that is my story. Now you know why the old rabbi is so strange, eh?"

"We don't think you're strange," Quinn said. "Honest."

"Well," Hector said, "we sorta did." He blushed. "Sorry."

"No need," Rabbi Shwartz said. "You know the truth of things, now. And that's all that matters."

He gestured to the piles of maps.

"I've been trying to follow them. Seeking out their lair. Golems like to come and go under the cover of night. Sewers, tunnels, and caves suit them best. Damp, dark places."

"I think we found one," Quinn said. "In the caves behind the Falls." He told the rabbi about their midnight adventure. The big man listened carefully, one hand idly stroking his steel gray beard.

"I was wondering what you were doing up there," he said. "I checked after you left. Before I got a chance to warn you."

"We're sorry," Wendy said. "We thought..."

"I know," the Rabbi said sadly.

"Did you see anything?" Hector asked.

"No," Rabbi Shwartz replied. "No tunnel. No golem."

"That's impossible," Quinn said. "It was there. I swear." Wendy and Hector nodded enthusiastically.

"They could have shut it. Golems are crafty, if their master makes them so."

"So now what do we do?" Wendy asked. "Those things are out there right now, and we're probably the only people in the world who know what's really going on!"

"We must think," the rabbi said. "First, you have to tell me what the golem that took Henry looked like."

Quinn did, finding it difficult to explain the horrifying creature in detail. It didn't sound anything like the ones from the rabbi's story.

"And did it have something carved on its chest?"

"Yes, but...I didn't understand it."

The rabbi slid a piece of paper and pencil his way. "Can you draw it? Or something close to it?"

Quinn wrote, and for the first time in a long while, cursed himself for quitting his Hebrew lessons. Still, he made the best copy he could, and slid it back.

כּוֹלְאִים

"Arrest," the rabbi said. "Or most likely, imprison. That's a new one. And it could explain why there were no markings on Randall or Martin when I saw them in the morgue."

"But what's it doing?" Hector asked.

"Exactly what's written on it," the rabbi said. "It's not killing them. It's...turning them. Imprisoning their living bodies in the clay. Making them its slaves."

"So we need to find this original one. Just like yours and Gotzner's," Quinn said.

"If we find it and destroy it, the ones it changed will return to their human selves," the rabbi said. "We *must* find it."

"And fast," Wendy added. "Before the whole town is...imprisoned."

"We must focus on patterns. Crimes, supernatural or not, always follow a pattern. It's just a matter of finding one." He looked down at his watch. "It's nearly nightfall. It will be hunting soon. We must catch it before it has a chance to strike."

Quinn thought hard about what he'd seen. "Well, we know the golem, the *original* golem, took Randall and Martin. Then Randall and Martin tried taking Gibbs. That night they probably got Terry, Hank, and Maria. And then they took my brother."

"Randall...Martin..." the Rabbi's bushy eyebrows furrowed like two dancing caterpillars. "Henry."

Quinn looked up at the rabbi, and saw the man was staring at the badge clutched in his hand.

"The Heroes of Stark River."

"Holy smoke!" Hector bleated.

"Holy smoke, indeed," the old man mused, tugging his gray beard. "Who else was with them?"

"Ethan Malman," Quinn said. "But he died, of course. And then there's—" He stopped. His brain felt like it had just been blasted with white fire. "Brent Foster!"

"The guy who lives in the woods?" Wendy asked. "Mom and dad always warned me to keep away from him."

"Same," Hector said.

Quinn shook his head. "Brent was never right after the accident. Henry and the other guys tried to get him out, tried to help him. But he shut himself away in that cabin. I can't even remember his face, really."

"But what about the kids?" Wendy asked. "What did they do? There's no pattern there."

"Maybe they were like poor Mr. Gibbs or Mr. Link," the Rabbi said. "And came across the creatures by accident. The wrong place and the wrong time." He furrowed his brow, deep in thought. "But Brent. Brent Foster."

He stood so suddenly his coffee toppled over, soaking the maps on the table.

"That's a good place to start," he said. "Come with me." He moved to a large chest in the corner.

The Crew stood by while he unlocked it. When he threw open the lid, they let out a collective gasp. Inside were dozens of chisels marked מת, along with the largest hammer Quinn had ever seen. The head was a chunk of iron the size of a cinder block. He wondered if he'd even be able to lift that thing.

"Take these," he said, handing out the sharpened chisels. Each of the kids took a handful, placing them in their backpacks.

"So, this book," Hector said, "the one that you can make a monster with," he swallowed. "You still have it?"

"It's here," the rabbi said, moving to one of the bookshelves.

He drew out a heavy looking wooden box. He opened it and let in a hissing breath.

"What?"

"It's...gone.". He held up the book and let the pages fall open. "The entire section."

"Oh, no," Hector whispered.

"We have little time," the rabbi said. "Tonight, we'll find the golem and destroy it once and for all."

"Where?" Hector asked.

"The cabin," Rabbi Shwartz said. "Brent Foster's cabin. The last victim on its list. Or so I hope."

Monster Hunters

The crew loaded their weapons into the back of the rabbi's car, an old woody that looked like it hadn't been driven in years. Hector checked the strings on their bows while Wendy wrote מת in bold letters on each of the arrows. Quinn rummaged through his backpack, now heavy with chisels, choosing an assortment of m-80's, and anything else with a strong enough blast to shatter clay. He also handed out ponchos and flashlights.

His dad's lessons on vigilance were paying off.

"You came prepared," Rabbi Shwartz said. "That's good." He placed his hammer on the passenger seat along with a burlap sack filled with chisels.

The rain began to fall in earnest as they left the synagogue. While the rest of the group discussed the plan, Quinn found himself lost in thought.

The idea of Henry becoming a golem made his heart ache. He couldn't help but picture him out there, lurching around with the others, his body still working but his mind gone. He wondered if he'd ever get him back. He wondered if he'd ever see his brother's smile again, or hear his voice. No more 'Hey, pal,' in the morning. No more John Wayne impressions. No more rides to the drive in, or quiet nights on the couch watching *Midnight Creature Feature* or *Nightmare Theater* with a bowl of popcorn.

No more lessons, Quinn thought, *the lessons that only big brothers can teach little ones.*

And if Henry were lost, *truly* lost, what would happen to Quinn? Loneliness crept up on him like a dull ache, with dread not far behind. Where would he live? He had an aunt, a great aunt Helen. She lived somewhere on Long Island. Quinn couldn't even bring her face to mind. Aside from Helen, he had no family. No one to take him in. Would they send him to an orphanage?

Like Oliver Twist, he thought, struggling not to cry in front of his friends.

No, his brave voice piped in. *Stop thinking like that. Henry isn't dead, and you're not alone. You can fix this. You and your friends, and the rabbi and Mr. Arpin and all the rest. There are good people in this world, people who stand against the dark. So stand with them, Quinn Katz, and pull yourself together*!

"Whoah!"

Quinn was thrown into the back of the driver's seat as the car screeched to a halt.

He saw the bright yellow glow of headlights through the windshield, and while he picked himself back up, Mr. Arpin's truck pulled alongside.

"Not a good night for a joy ride, rabbi!" He called over the pounding rain.

"It's not a particularly joyous ride," the rabbi answered, and Quinn saw Mr. Arpin's grin widen.

"Who you got back there?" he asked, leaning a bit out of the window.

Quinn looked to Wendy and Hector, unsure if they should hide themselves. The last thing they needed was Dr. Delgado or Mr. Francis finding out about this.

"The children are helping, Jacques. I think I know where the gol—" He caught himself, "Where the Snatcher will strike next."

Mr. Arpin's grin disappeared.

"They're kids, rabbi."

"Yes. And tougher than you know."

"That so? Well they don't scare easily, and that's for sure."

"Listen," the rabbi said, "I know what we're dealing with, here. And I know how to stop it. But I can't do it alone. You and the others are still patrolling, yes?"

"Sure," he said. "I'm on the south side. Wayne Todd's up near the mill and the lumberyard. And...hey, Wendy!" He waved. "Your dad's up at the station, covering the woods and the Falls."

"Good," the rabbi said. "We're heading to Brent Foster's place. Have you heard from him?"

"Crazy Brent?" Arpin shook his head. "Haven't seen him in months. Delivered some firewood to him in November, that was it. What's he got to do with this?"

"Maybe everything," the rabbi said, "and I need to get there as soon as I can."

"Here." Arpin moved his truck closer and handed the rabbi a radio. "We had a spare, and we need all the help we can get. You keep in contact. We're on channel two. Let us know what you find. We'll do the same."

"Thank you." The rabbi moved to put the car in gear, paused. "Stay on the lookout, Jacques. And if you see anything suspicious, don't try to take it on alone."

"Will do," he said. "And you do the same."

"And don't tell our parents!" Hector pleaded from the backseat. "Please!"

Mr. Arpin laughed and gave a wave. "No worries on that count. You just be safe, stick close to Rabbi Shwartz."

Brent Foster's cabin was inaccessible by car. Only a narrow trail through the woods led to his small plot. The group slogged their way through the drenched forest. The Crypt Crew had their bows at the ready, arrows notched, full quivers over their shoulders. Rabbi Shwartz took the lead, hammer and chisel in hand.

They emerged from a tangle of brush and into Brent Foster's yard. It was littered with rusted machinery, trash, and what looked like department store mannequins, each one riddled with bullet holes.

The cabin itself was small, more of a hut, some of the windows were covered in plastic instead of glass. A sad place. Quinn had never really known Brent, even though he'd been one of Henry's closest friends. The accident changed him. The river, too. While Henry relived it in his nightmares, it seemed Brent did the same, only awake. He never left this place.

"Brent! Brent Foster!" Rabbi Shwartz yelled at the front door.

They waited, ponchos drenched beneath battering rain. There was no answer.

The rabbi threw his shoulder against the door, hinges giving easily under his weight.

Brent Foster lived in a single room. Quinn saw a wood burning stove and an ice box on one side, with a small sink and one of those tables that folds down from the wall. On the other side of the room was a ratty mattress and a television with a cracked screen.

Globs of clay dripped from the ceiling, ran runny down the walls, lay slick and sludgy underfoot.

"Too late," Wendy said.

Rabbi Shwartz let out a frustrated growl. He stalked around the cabin, searching.

"There!"

A set of inhumanly long footprints, and behind them, two lines. The golem's feet, and Brent's as he was being dragged. They led out the back door.

Quinn followed them, but the rain was falling in heavy sheets and the lawn outside had turned into a churning bog of mud. The prints vanished, as they had for Randall.

And Martin.

And Henry.

Once again, the golem had escaped.

A loud squeak from the portable radio burst through the room, sending even the rabbi jumping in surprise.

"Fellas, it's Dale. I'm up at the Falls. Going to check something out."

Wendy ran closer. "Dad!"

"Tell us what you see," came Mr. Arpin's voice.

"Something..." the radio made a static, warbling sound. "Yeah, it's a person, alright. Up near the first cave."

"Wait for us," Mr. Arpin said.

The Crew gathered around the rabbi, the radio clutched in his hands.

A minute passed before Dale Francis' voice came back over the radio waves.

"Hey!" he said, " that looks like...it's...my God...*Henry*!"

Quinn leapt for the radio, but Rabbi Shwartz pushed him back.

"Wait," he hissed.

"But if he's there—"

The rabbi held up a finger, demanding silence.

Dale's voice returned. "He's up in that cave. I can see him clear through the rain." When he spoke again, his voice sounded far away, like he let the radio wander from his lips. "Henry? It's Dale! We've been looking all over for you! What are you doing there? Come on out of there...I got an extra rain slicker in the truck."

Silence.

"Well?" Mr. Arpin asked.

"Dale?"

"Hey!" Dale cried. "Henry, come back!"

Finally, the rabbi lifted the radio to his lips. "Dale, it's Rabbi Shwartz."

"Rabbi? How'd you get in on this?"

"He's got the kids with him," Arpin said.

"The kids?" Dale sounded confused.

"Listen, Dale. Don't go in those caves. No matter what you see. You wait for me, understand?"

"Huh?" Dale's confusion was clear over the static. "But he's right there!"

"Dale, listen to me. It's too dangerous. Wait until—"

"Henry!"

Silence.

"Dale?" The Rabbi said. "DALE!"

"I'm up in the cave. First one. He's a few yards ahead. Hey, Henry! Stop! Hey, it's okay. What's wrong?"

Wendy took the radio from the rabbi. "Dad?" she said. "Dad, it's me. Don't go any further! Please listen to me. *Please*!"

"Don't you worry, I'm fine." Silence. "Wait. Hey! Henry's coming back. Henry?" Static. "He looks—" Static. "Oh my G—"

"Dad!" Wendy screamed, clutching the radio. "DAD, RUN!"

Mr. Francis' scream roared through the speaker.

"Dad? Dad!" Wendy shook the radio. Started beating it with her fist. Her face twisted in a mask of pain. "Dad please, please get out of there!"

Wendy was still clutching the radio. No more voices came through. Just the low hiss of static. She sniffled, turning away from them to wipe her tears. Hector put his arm around her shoulder, giving Quinn a grave look.

"Come," the rabbi said, hoisting his hammer. "We will end this tonight."

They found Mr. Francis' truck on the gravel road, not too far from where the Crew had hidden their bikes when they'd first explored the caves. The truck was still running, floodlights illuminating the base of the Falls where the weathered stones formed the steps leading to Dead Man's Rest. The rain had stopped, humidity ushering in a thick blanket of fog.

Rabbi Shwartz parked and sat for a moment, drumming his fingers on the steering wheel, his face tight in thought.

The Crew got themselves ready. Quinn handed out the bows, making sure each arrow was fitted with a heavy stone tip marked and blessed by the rabbi. Hector gathered the fireworks and made sure to take a box of waterproof matches. He slung an UNCLE SAM'S THUNDERBOLT behind his quiver and stuffed his pockets with m-80's. Wendy taped flashlights to the bows and ran to her dad's truck, returning with his ranger hat on her head.

"You look ready," the rabbi said approvingly. "Are you?"

"My Dad's in there," Wendy said, sticking a few chisels into her belt loop.

"And Henry," Quinn said, his voice shaking.

"And Maria," Hector said.

The rabbi reached into the trunk and produced four lanterns. "Take these," he said. "In case the flashlights fail."

Quinn lifted the lantern, feeling its weight. His back was already burdened by the heavy quiver of arrows and the bow, along with the fireworks and chisels. But in that moment, it all felt light as a feather. Adrenaline had taken over. He looked to the Falls. All he could see was Henry.

The rabbi led the way up into the caves. Quinn was surprised at how nimble he was, climbing up the stone stairway with ease, even with his wooden leg.

"I never thought I'd be doing this again," the rabbi huffed, as if reading Quinn's thoughts.

They came to the opening in the wall. It wasn't covered by a mucus-like layer of clay and mud like before. It stood open, a second yawning cave mouth ready to swallow them up. The rabbi raised his lantern.

"Crafty. This was not here the night I looked."

The tunnel had grown. A few nights ago it was barely tall enough to stand in. Now it was at least ten feet high, and just as wide.

"Someone's been busy," Wendy said.

"Geeze," Hector breathed. He shivered, hugging himself in the coolness of the cave.

Rabbi Shwartz stepped into the tunnel. "*The Book of Gotzner* contained many secrets. Golems are just one of the mysteries he uncovered. There are ways to move the earth itself. The pages ripped from the book contained other incantations. The thief has dangerous knowledge. Ways to summon and awaken sheddim. *Demons*."

Quinn remembered the way the tunnel seemed alive. The way the walls seemed to expand and contract like lungs. The way the mud curled around his feet, as if aware of his presence.

The memory of the thing that grabbed his ankles flashed in his brain like a flare. He aimed the bow at the ground. The mud was ankle deep. The lantern hanging from his belt lent its light. He was glad that if something were hiding in here, it'd have a very hard time *staying* hidden.

They continued down the sloping tunnel, avoiding the hanging stalactites that dripped ice-cold water onto the hoods of their ponchos. Quinn felt himself growing cold, like they were walking in brisk autumn air.

They must have gone deep. The air smelled different. Stale. He wondered if air could go bad, and remembered Hector's joke about bringing a parakeet, like the miners used to. It'd be hard to tell if air was running out, and he didn't think golems needed it.

If they got woozy or sluggish from lack of oxygen, they wouldn't be much good facing off against clay monsters.

A cry drifted through the dark.

"Dad!" Wendy sprinted forward.

"Wait!"

Rabbi Shwartz grabbed for her, but she was too quick.

She hurdled down into the tunnel, lantern swinging wildly.

The rest of the crew followed, running after her as the sounds of screams and struggle grew louder.

The tunnel forked, and luckily Wendy wasn't too far ahead. They followed her light and slid down steeper and steeper where the tunnel turned colder and muddier, until Quinn lost his footing and fell hard on his backside, sliding down in front of the rabbi and Hector before slamming hard into the side wall. The rabbi lifted him by the scruff of his poncho and set him upright.

The tunnel opened into a wide cavern. Wendy stood in the center, slowly backing away as two golems shambled forward, their arms outstretched, mouths opening, eyes yellow and...*hungry*, Quinn thought.

But these two weren't human. They were smaller, shriveled looking, and had the same long, tentacle-like arms of the original golem. Their faces looked like dried apples, warped and wrinkled, with mud dripping from their eye sockets. Each of them bore Hebrew on their chests, but Quinn couldn't read it.

"What do they say?" He asked.

"Defend," the Rabbi answered.

Defend? Defend what?

"Those bows," he said. "You've had practice with them?"

Quinn and Hector shared a look.

"Not really," Hector said. "We practiced in the afternoon."

"An *afternoon*?"

Quinn remembered how many times he'd hit his target. It was easy, standing in the backyard, aiming at wood cutouts of Dracula, Freddy

Kruger, and Frankenstein's monster. But now he was in a dark cavern, and the shriveled, shambling golems were edging closer. Moving targets.

Targets that fought back.

"Nock your arrows, boys. And make sure the points are marked."

Quinn slid an arrow, the stone point marked DEATH, onto the bow. He raised it against his cheek.

"I'll take the left," he told Hector.

"I...I don't know if I can do this."

"Just aim," Quinn told him. "Pretend we're in my yard."

Hector nocked his arrow, arms trembling as he hefted the bow.

Wendy joined them. The rabbi moved, placing himself in front of her like a shield. He drew a bottle of lantern oil from his coat.

"Hector, hand me those matches."

The two golems lurched forward, arms outstretched, impossibly long fingers moving like tentacles. They made those strange chittering sounds, jaws unhinging as they neared. Mud and clay dripped down their shriveled chins like drool, filling the cavern with that nasty sewer stench.

The Rabbi took the bottle and shook it out, sending lantern oil splattering on the ground between them.

He flicked a match alight...

"Begone!"

Threw it.

The cavern floor ignited in a brilliant blaze. Quinn shielded his eyes, nearly blinded, nostrils filled with the pungent stink of burning oil. He looked between his fingers and watched as the golems drew back from the flames, screeching like wounded animals.

"Now!" The Rabbi thundered. "Aim for the chest!"

Quinn drew back on the bowstring, shoulder flaring in pain as he pulled it back as far as he could.

"Fire!"

The arrows loosed, whining as they sailed through the air. It happened so fast Quinn could barely see it.

Two loud *cracks* as the stone points marked מת pierced through the golems' chests.

Otherworldly shrieks followed. The monsters staggered back, and as they did the rabbi leaped over the flames. He didn't hesitate. Didn't give them any time to gather themselves. As one fell back, he drew out his hammer and gave the final blow, pushing Quinn's arrowhead further into the monster's chest like a nail into a coffin.

The second golem had fallen down on its back, wriggling in the mud. The rabbi stood over it. But before he could drive the arrow home, the golem let out one last garbled hiss, and broke. It fell apart like a crumbling cake, piece by piece, until it was just a pile of dried clay.

The Crew watched in awe as the rabbi stood over the heap, burning lantern oil slowly extinguishing in the mud.

"You did it!" Wendy cried. "You did it, guys. *Nobody* messes with the Crypt Crew!"

Hector stood motionless, his bow still hefted in firing position. "I... actually hit one?"

"Don't celebrate so soon," the rabbi said. He peered down, reading the Hebrew on the fallen creature's cracked and crumbling chest. "Defend," he murmured.

"Defending what?" Wendy asked.

He gestured with his hammer. Beyond the slain golems was a door set into the cavern wall. It was iron, red with rust, and covered in mold. Written across the top in blocky white paint was a single word:

אמת
EMETH.

"The lair," the rabbi said. "We've found it."

The Golem and the Pit

"Whatever we find behind this door," the rabbi said, "we must have courage."

Quinn swallowed hard. Evil, *true* evil, was waiting for them. He looked to Hector and Wendy, their faces and clothes smeared in mud, shivering in the cold of the cave.

Rabbi Shwartz pulled the iron door. It let out a groaning creak as it opened into the cavern, spilling light from the inner chamber.

Cautiously, the group made their way inside.

Quinn felt something familiar about the place. It was a basement. He knew that much, since there was a steep wooden staircase leading up to a door. In one corner was an ancient looking boiler, covered in rust and making a slight clanging noise, then a *thud*, as if there was something trapped inside and trying to get out.

Quinn studied the old machine, and the heaps of boxes that surrounded it.

A boiler.

"Guys," he said quietly.

Hector and Wendy moved further inside the room, stepping around heaps of boxes until Hector let out a loud hiss.

Beneath the dust, Quinn could make out **OLD WEST BOW AND ARROW SET** printed on the side.

"It can't be…" Wendy said softly. "There's no way that tunnel stretched from the Falls to…to *here*."

"It did."

The rabbi pointed to the far wall, where a plastic tarp hung like a curtain. A large doorway had been cut into the earthen wall. Above, just like the iron door in the cavern, the word EMETH was scrawled over the tarp.

The basement was littered with heaps of stones and dirt. Piles of it were built up around the corners, along with pickaxes, buckets of gravel, and a few mud-caked shovels.

The piles grew taller as they approached the tarp. The rabbi held up a hand.

"Nice and quiet," he mouthed. "No sudden moves. No matter what you see. Understood?"

The Crew nodded. Quinn felt that familiar numbness taking hold of his hands and feet, that creeping grip of panic and terror, and tried to stamp it down.

They passed through the tarp and entered a place beyond words.

Beyond sanity.

Torches and lanterns burned, casting an orange-tinged light around the cavernous room. In the center was a great pit, at least fifteen feet deep. The walls and floors were beds of bright red clay. In one corner, resting on a ratty cot, was the original golem, its long, skinny arms wrapped around itself like a bat sheltering beneath its leathery wings. Beside it, sitting in a chair and reading from the *Stark Falls Minuteman*, was Mr. Malman. A long table stood next to the chair. A record was spinning, the volume low as he spoke.

"And so," Mr. Malman read, "with Deputy Katz missing, what will the town council do? The Snatcher has taken his third victim and is likely responsible for the kidnapping of three children. With local law enforcement gone, I fear for the safety of Stark Falls. Next issue, I plan to release the names of all suspects, with or without the approval of Deputy Katz." He folded up the paper, patting the golem on its enormous foot. "You've done a fine job, my wonderful, wonderful boy. You're the talk of the town!"

The golem let out a chirping sound, squirming like a happy child after a good bedtime story.

Above the golem's cot, a framed picture was hung on the earthen wall.

Ethan Malman.

Malman ran a hand over the golem's face. "Oh, my boy. I'm so happy you're back. We have much work ahead of us. Much work. But first you need your rest, don't you? Here, let papa put on your favorite, so you can dream sweet dreams."

Malman got up and went to the record player. He slid a new album from its case, set the record on the table, and dropped the needle.

"'Glow Worm" lilted from the speaker.

"That was him," Wendy whispered as they crouched down behind a large pile of rubble. "The one that kept calling the radio station."

"And you!" Mr. Malman's voice carried over the music. "You should all get comfortable. I hope I've made the grave large enough!"

Quinn peeked over the rubble, watching as Malman moved to the edge of the pit.

Below, he could hear sloshing and a chorus of low moans.

A wooden plank had been laid over the pit. Malman stepped onto it, hands behind his back, and walked slowly across. He peered down, a maniacal smile on his face.

"Oh, hush now," he cooed. "We're not quite finished. You'll have more grave mates, soon enough. Ah!" His voice was suddenly jubilant. "How are you down there, Mr. Harwich? Is our favorite reporter getting a good scoop?"

A muffled, garbled groan echoed from the pit.

Quinn dared another look. Across the chamber, the golem was still on the cot, its arms slithering and curling like contented snakes. Malman turned and walked back to the record player. As he did so, the rabbi stood from their hiding place.

"Jonas!"

Malman paused.

"Oh, rabbi!" He turned, eyes strangely bright.

Rabbi Shwartz stepped towards the pit, hammer and chisel ready.

"Jonas, what have you done?"

"Something no one else could do. I brought my son back."

The record skipped on the player.

The golem stirred.

"That," the rabbi pointed with the hammer, "Is not Ethan. You must stop. This is a dark thing."

"And who possessed such knowledge to begin with? Hmm? You. You're part of this, now. What do you think will happen when people find out who owned the *Book of Gotzner*?"

"You stole it," the rabbi said. "Stole it to create this...this monster."

"HE IS MY SON!

The golem was up, now, the claws at the end of its arms leaving deep gauges in the clay floor as it moved closer to Mr. Malman.

Quinn stood. "Please, Mr. Malman. That's not Ethan."

Malman reeled. "Quinn? What are you..." He stared daggers at the rabbi. "Why have you brought him here? This is no place for him."

"He brought us, too!" Wendy and Hector joined him, wielding their bows, arrows trained on the golem.

"No!" Malman cried, voice choking with rage and fear. "You will not hurt my son!"

"It must be done," the rabbi said softly. "It cannot exist in this world."

"Of course it can!" Malman snapped. "And you will not take it from me. Do you know how long I toiled, down in the muck and the mire, creating one failure after another? How my heart broke each time a new golem failed?" He shook his head. "But this time, I did what the book said. It *is* Ethan, you see. There's a part of Ethan inside of him."

Quinn remembered the rabbi's story. Gotzner had unearthed the grave of the young boy and used a part of him. That's how the golem truly came to life.

Malman ran a hand over the golem's hideous face and smiled. "My boy. My perfect, beautiful boy. He's come back to me."

"Ethan's grave," Quinn said. "You said someone had vandalized it. Tried to dig him up. That was you!"

"Yes," Malman said. "And that worthless brother of yours hadn't the slightest idea."

Anger flared through Quinn's veins. No one talked about Henry like that.

"Where are they?" Quinn demanded. "Where are the ones you turned?"

"They're right here," Malman said. "Waiting for the others."

Quinn edged forward. In the bottom of the pit, he saw the missing people of Stark Falls. Randall and Martin. Frank and Terry. Brent and Maria. Mr. Francis. He spotted others, too. Mr. Birch, the hardware store owner. Mr. Todd, the library custodian. And there, surrounded by members of the Garden Club, was old Mrs. Ruane, her ear trumpet now glued to the side of her clay-covered head.

They were walking around blindly, groping walls and stumbling like mindless robots.

How many more people would end up in that pit if they couldn't stop him?

"Why?" Quinn asked. "Why would you do this?"

"Because they came back," Mr. Malman spat. "And my Ethan didn't."

"It wasn't their fault!"

"I don't care!" Malman thundered. "That day on the river, everyone came home. Every. Single. Boy. Except for mine. How is that for justice, eh? How's that for *faith*?"

"You defiled his grave," the rabbi said. "Dishonored him. After he gave his life saving those children."

"Dishonored?" Malman let out a laugh. "I brought him back. I resurrected him. Made him in a better image. A more cunning image. More dangerous. One that could take those lucky sons who survived, while mine came back in a box!"

"Enough!" Rabbi Shwartz thundered, and charged.

Malman threw himself out of the way as the rabbi tackled the golem. The monster let out a shriek, spraying wet clay from its mouth as the rabbi swung his hammer. The long arms wrapped around the rabbi's wrist, and the hammer dropped from his hand.

"No!"

The golem gripped the rabbi by the neck and hoisted him up. His eyes bulged as he struggled for breath. The creature was Quinn's height and incredibly skinny, but so strong that it held the rabbi up like he was nothing more than a toy. It opened its mouth, spat a glob of wet clay into the rabbi's face, and hurled him across the room. The rabbi crashed into the wall.

The Crew was halfway across the pit.

"Children." Malman stood at the opposite end. Behind him, the golem waited, its tentacle arms outstretched. "This isn't how I wanted this to go."

"Oh, no? How did you want it to go? You think you can take our families away from us, and *what*...everything would go back to normal?"

"Yes," Malman said simply. "If the rabbi over there hadn't caught on, that's exactly what I wanted. My boy would be back, the ones who left him to die would be gone and buried, and you, my children, would be with me. Safe and sound. Where no one could judge you, or harass you, or hurt you. You were to be mine. And the other children, Terry and Hank and the rest of those horrible brats, they wouldn't trouble you any longer. Not when I have Ethan fill in the pit for good."

"We're *not* yours," Hector said. The louder he spoke, the more his voice cracked and trembled. "And that's not your son. It's a monster."

"Just like you," Wendy said. She pulled her bowstring back tight. "Give me my Dad. *Now*."

Malman raised a foot over the plank. "You're really so intent on joining the others, hm?" His icy eyes fell on Wendy. "Your father, who pays you so little attention that you dream of running to New York? And you, Hector. Do you really think you'll miss your sister's abuses? The beatings? The bruises? The humiliation?" He gestured to his right eye and the horrible, deep purple bruise around the socket. "A parting gift. Your sister did not go quietly." He held out his arms. "By all means...join her."

He slammed a boot down onto the plank. Quinn staggered. Hector lost his footing, fell backwards. He reached out, grabbed a hold of Quinn and Wendy, and in a split second they were all falling together.

Quinn smacked hard onto the wet clay, air squeezed from his lungs. He opened his eyes and saw Randall Colburn standing over him, looking down with those yellow eyes. Quinn rolled out of the way just in time as the heavy foot sank deep into the clay, missing his head by centimeters.

"Dad, please! It's me!"

Wendy and Hector were back to back, fending off Mr. Francis and Maria.

Mr. Francis' mouth was open, spraying a continuous stream of clay, trying to cover Wendy. She edged backwards, holding her torn poncho above her like an umbrella. "Stop!" she cried. "Don't you recognize me?"

Mr. Francis paused for a moment, cocked his head, and in a blindingly quick motion, swiped at her with a giant clay fist. Before it connected, Hector dove and pushed her away. Mr. Francis' wild swing threw him off balance, and he fell.

Maria stepped over Mr. Francis and advanced on Hector, who scooted in the mud as quickly as he could.

"Maria, don't do this," he cried, his face awash in mud and terror. "Don't...don't give in. I'm here to help."

Quinn looked up out of the pit. There had to be a way to get out. If not, they were goners.

"We have to get up!" he called.

Two powerful hands grabbed his shoulders, pulled him back, propelled him forward. He careened into the wall, his nose smacking into the hard-packed clay.

Spots and stars dotted his vision as he turned, and came face to face with Henry.

His big brother looked down, his face mean and nasty like some sick joke. Quinn leapt backwards as Henry swiped at him, trying to grip his poncho.

It struck him that the last conversation he'd ever had with Henry had been an argument. If this didn't go right, those would be the last words the Katz brothers shared.

Quinn couldn't allow that.

Martin loomed behind them, reaching down for Quinn, his hands grasping for his neck.

"Hector!" He cried, searching the pit until he saw his friend scooting on his butt as Maria limped toward him like a zombie.

"The bombs!"

"The what?"

"Fireworks!" Quinn cried, rolling to dodge Martin's foot. He looked around wildly for an escape.

And that's when he saw it.

A way out.

"Hector, light them off!"

"I can't...can't get to them!" He was scrambling away from his sister and her open mouth spewing clay.

Quinn stood, slicking himself off. Henry was to his right, Martin to the left. Hector was dead ahead, up against the wall with Maria closing in slowly but surely.

Quinn had a clearing.

He ran, could feel the air *whoosh* in his ears as Martin and Henry both dove for him. He cast a quick look back, watching as the two smacked their heads together and stumbled.

He slid to a stop beside Hector, knocking Maria off balance.

"We need a distraction," he said. "The rabbi did it with the lantern oil. Those m-80's should do the trick."

"Can't reach…" Hector was pushed so far against the wall of the pit that his backpack was completely lodged in it.

Randall made that familiar chittering sound, his arms held up in front of him like Frankenstein's monster.

"I got it!"

Quinn dug into his own backpack. He pulled out an arrowhead and began work slicing the straps from Hector's shoulders.

Hector squirmed away as Quinn yanked the backpack from the wall and Randall staggered forward. Hector got behind him and gave a powerful shove, sending him face first into the wall. Randall struggled to free himself from the clay, but the shove was strong enough that Quinn thought he'd be stuck there for a while. Long enough for them to make their escape, at least.

"Okay," he said, looking over his shoulder, where Martin and Henry had both seemed to shake off their head smacks. "We light these and throw them at their feet."

"I'm shaking too bad, Q. What if it doesn't work?"

"It will."

"And what then?"

"Then," Quinn pointed to the walls of the pit. "We climb."

Hector swallowed.

"We can do it," Quinn said. "It's like the climbing wall at the Falls."

Hector shook his head. "Quinn, you know I never even made it two feet off the ground. And there weren't golems chasing me."

Maria lurched up from the muddy floor, gurgling and growling.

"Guys!"

They watched as Wendy pushed her father away with her bow, now cracked in two. She was swinging the pieces of it wildly back and forth, fending off savage swipes.

"Hang on!" Quinn called. "You have those matches, right?"

Hector dug into his pockets and pulled out two plastic bags. "Kept 'em dry this time."

Mrs. Ruane let out a garbled shriek, reaching out to throttle Quinn's throat.

They lit the m-80's. The pit filled with the stench of sulfur.

"Now!"

The fireworks plopped into the ground. Quinn held his breath, thinking for a moment that the fuses had gone out. But before he could say anything, two loud cracks blasted, and the pit shook. Mrs. Ruane flew backwards, knocking into the rest of the Garden Club.

"Let's go!"

Quinn grabbed Hector by the arm and ran for the opposite end of the pit, where Wendy was still fighting against her dad. Together, they pulled Mr. Francis back. He fell like a toppled oak, slamming deep into the clay.

"Come on," Quinn said. He jumped up and sank his hands deep into the wall, digging out handholds. It was like climbing up a cliff made of jelly. Little by little, hand by foot, he inched his way upward.

Hector and Wendy followed, using the holes Quinn had dug out in his wake. Below, Quinn could hear the chitterings of the golems.

"I can't do it!" Hector cried. Quinn dared a look down and saw him struggling.

"You can!" Quinn said. "You *have* to!"

He reached the top, his hand slamming down onto hard-packed dirt. He hoisted himself up, then flopped over on his belly to give Hector and Wendy a helping hand.

Finally, the Crypt Crew freed, found themselves panting on the floor of the Malman & Son's cellar. Quinn crawled forward, looking down at Henry. His brother was walking in slow, rigid circles, completely devoid of anything resembling Henry Katz. His heart broke.

"You know," Hector said beside him, looking down at Maria, "Even when she's like...like that. I couldn't do it, Q. I couldn't even push her away." He buried his face on the earthen floor. "What are we gonna *do*?"

"Kids."

The voice was faint.

Quinn found Rabbi Shwartz propped up in the corner, his wooden leg shattered. He held the massive hammer in one hand. The other was against his chest. A faint trickle of blood ran through his fingers.

Across from the rabbi, Brent Foster was impaled against the wall, a chisel sticking out of his shoulder. He waved his arms, clay dribbling from his cracked lips.

"Rabbi!"

He knelt beside him, and saw the old man's chest rise and fall, his breath coming out in ragged waves.

"They fled...into the cave." Behind them, Brent let out a frustrated groan. Quinn winced at the sound.

"Brent is fine." He keeled to the side, the hammer dropping to the ground at Quinn's feet. "You have to finish it."

Quinn stared down at the weapon.

"But," he said, "I can't even lift that."

The rabbi coughed violently. "You can do anything you set your mind to, Quinn Katz. All of you. I've always believed that. I still believe that. The hammer is only as heavy as you make it. If you believe, you can wield it. You're the only ones who can stop this. Save your family and friends. He won't stop. He'll keep taking and taking, until Stark Falls is nothing but a town full of monsters."

"We can't do it without you, rabbi," Quinn said. He took the man's hand in his own and squeezed it, fighting back tears.

All those years I spent being afraid of this man, he thought. *Why? What was it all for?*

He looked into the rabbi's eyes and saw nothing but love. Encouragement. Belief.

"You have to," the rabbi said. "I know you're scared." He let out a wet cough. "I was too. It's okay to be scared. But don't let fear run your life. Fear can choke the mind and drain the heart. You have big hearts. All of you." He nudged the hammer closer to Quinn. "Jonas Malman is not a bad man. Not truly. He's just a man who lost his son and decided to turn to vengeance. Grief...a father's grief...can be a terrible thing. Don't hold vengeance in your hearts. Ever."

The rabbi closed his eyes, letting out a deep, rattling sigh.

"No!" Wendy threw herself next to him, wrapping her arms around his neck. "Rabbi, no!"

Quinn stared down, terrified.

He wasn't...

He couldn't be...

"Kids." The rabbi's voice startled them. "I'm not dead. Just tired."

A hint of a smile spread across his ashen face. "But that might not be true for long. Go, now. Find them."

Quinn bent down and gripped the hammer, his fingers running over the worn leather straps. He took a deep breath, knees buckling, and while the sweat poured down his brow, realized that he'd lifted it.

"Wow," Wendy said. "You're like Conan the Barbarian! Hector, did you see that?" Hector was still peering over at the pit, shaking his head.

Quinn's shoulders were already aching, and he struggled to keep his arms from trembling. "Sure don't feel like him."

"Even so," Wendy said, "They couldn't have gone far." She paused, turning back to Rabbi Shwartz. "We'll send help as soon as we can."

"Don't worry about me," he said. "Find the golem. Destroy the shem."

Wendy nodded, drawing the last of her chisels from her belt.

"We will," she said. "And that's a Crypt Crew promise."

The rabbi shook his head. "I don't know what that means, but I believe you, Ms. Francis." He gave a small wink, then settled back against the wall.

Hector and Wendy looked to Quinn. The hammer felt like a thousand pounds.

"This is my last one," Wendy said, handing Quinn the chisel marked מת.

"Well," Quinn said, hoisting the hammer up onto his shoulder. "Better make it count."

Two moans drew their attention back to the pit. Terry and Frank had managed to climb up, their clay covered bodies heaving as they pulled themselves over the edge.

"Go," the Rabbi said, shifting. "I'll deal with them."

Hector and Wendy gathered the two remaining lanterns, and with Quinn in the lead, the Crew made their way back into the darkness of the caves.

Showdown

Quinn paused to look at the crumbled golems just outside the iron door. He touched a piece of the cracked clay with his foot and watched it crumble to dust.

"I still can't believe it," Hector said quietly.

"Me neither," Quinn said. "Golems were always just stories. Legends. Like leprechauns in Ireland or the Hidden People in Iceland. I never knew about...about all this." He swept his arm around the heaps of crumbled earth. "Never in a million years did I think it was real."

"The rabbi should never have kept that book," Wendy said.

"I think he was trying to keep it safe," Quinn said. "And I think he was confident no one would trouble with that stuff. He said so himself. Why else would he move up here, in the middle of nowhere?"

"Well," Hector said, "I guess even in the middle of nowhere, there's always someone waiting."

"Mr. Malman. He really thinks he brought Ethan back," Wendy said sadly.

"He's in pain," Quinn said. Hector and Wendy fell silent. "Come on. We have to catch up." He led the way, feeling the weight of the hammer pull him down like an anchor. It was getting heavy. So heavy.

Halfway up the tunnel, a sound drew them to the side of the wall.

Static hissed through the mud. Wendy reached down and yanked a radio out of the muck.

"My dad's," she said. "It must be."

"Can you get a signal? Try and call Mr. Arpin?"

Wendy used her sleeve to clean out the speaker and clear the dials, then fiddled with the antenna. But as soon as she pulled it out, it bent, and the static ended abruptly. She shook her head.

"Just as well," Hector said. "Rabbi said it was up to us, didn't he? We're the ones for the job. Last line of defense."

Quinn studied him for a moment, noticing how Hector was suddenly carrying himself with more confidence. The confidence he'd always pretended to have before this whole mess had started.

"What?" he asked, noticing Quinn's look.

"Nothing. It's just…good to have you back. The old Hector."

Even in the dark of the tunnel, he could see Hector's cheeks flush as they continued on.

"Well," he said, "I'm good at Space Invaders, not fighting. I'll admit I wasn't too keen on this whole monster hunting." He paused, rubbing the back of his neck. "I mean, I *was*, until we…you know…"

"Ran into *actual* monsters?" Wendy asked.

Hector nodded.

"What changed?"

"It's…it's stupid."

"Really," Wendy urged. "What?"

"Well, it's you guys. If it was me alone, I don't think I would've made it. I couldn't have stopped Maria. Not like that. I think I would've just rolled over and let her change me. But when we're together…I don't know. I can believe in myself." He nodded to Quinn. "Like climbing up out of that pit. You know how many times I dreamed about climbing the rock wall at the Falls? How many times I sat back and watched all the other kids do it, pretending I sprained my ankle, or had a sour stomach? Man, I wished I could climb like everyone else. And tonight, I did."

"You always could," Quinn said. "Like you always say, you're a tough hombre."

"Only as tough as my friends."

"The Crypt Crew sticks together," Quinn said. "And when this is all over, I think we're gonna have a seriously scary story to tell."

"Yeah," Hector said. "But let's make sure we're around to tell it, okay?"

The three friends nodded.

Grave Robber's Way opened up before them. Quinn took the lead, staying low, crouching behind the jagged stalactites reaching up from the limestone floor.

Two figures stood on the jutting rock of the Diving Board, shrouded in mist-shot moonlight. Hector and Wendy snuffed out the lanterns.

"Oh, my Ethan. They wanted to hurt you. I'll never let them hurt you. Never ever again."

The golem chittered. Quinn edged around the rock to get a better look. Mr. Malman was on one knee beside it, his hand resting on the creature's head.

The golem reached up with its long claw, lightly touching Malman's cheek.

In the shadow, it really *did* look like a father comforting a child, but through the shaft of light in the waterfall, when Quinn looked close and *really* saw, the scene was something from a nightmare. The golem was injured, it seemed, and moved in slow, sluggish motions, its claws scraping loudly against the stone. The Rabbi must have put up a good fight.

"We'll be alright," Malman said. "We just need to get you somewhere safe."

Clang!

Quinn's blood ran cold as the hammer slipped from his hands. Malman shot up, the golem following suit.

"What do we do?" Hector whispered.

Beside him, Wendy brandished the chisel. Her eyes were fierce as she looked to Quinn.

"Go!" He heard Malman tell the golem. Thumping footfalls filled the cave.

Quinn picked up the hammer and ran out from behind the stalactite.

"Mr. Malman!" he called, his voice quivering. "It's us!"

Malman held out a hand. The golem paused mid-step. Its long, noodle-thin arms dropped to its sides, head nodding as it wavered from side to side like some sort of sleeping spell had been cast over it.

Quinn lifted the hammer over his head so Malman could see.

"You have to stop this," he told him.

"It's gone too far," Wendy said, stepping beside him.

"Please, Mr. Malman," Hector implored.

"Kids," Mr. Malman said, stepping closer, "you wouldn't hurt me, would you?"

Quinn looked from the old man to the golem. "No one wants to hurt anyone. But that thing—"

"*Thing*?" Malman snapped. "That *thing* is my son."

The golem lifted its head.

"You don't know what it's like," Mr. Malman said, "having the only thing, the only person in your life that made it worth living, gone."

"I do," Quinn said. "Henry and I lost our parents. You were there. You sat shiva with us!"

"Henry," Mr. Malman said. "Your wonderful Henry, the deputy. He came back. Martin and Randall. Even Brent." He shook his head.

"They saved people," Wendy said. "Doesn't that count?"

"What would *you* know about it?" Malman roared. "None of you know. None of you have any *idea*!"

"I know you're in pain," Quinn said. "And I know you made a mistake."

Malman's face darkened. "The only mistake I made was waiting this long to bring my son back."

Quinn pointed the hammer at the golem. "It isn't Ethan! We know about the *Book of Gotzner*. The rabbi told us everything. Mr. Malman, what you did...it's evil."

"It's *Ethan*!" Malman screeched.

"Don't you understand?" Quinn asked. "Mr. Malman, you said we were like your children. Taking Henry, taking Wendy's dad and Hector's sister—"

"It *had* to be done," Malman said. "Henry was always on the list. Dale just got in the way. And why would you care?" He pointed at Wendy. "The man forgets his own *daughter* exists! And Maria? Her and her little friends terrorized you. They scrawled hateful things on my shop walls and the synagogue. Stole from me. Laughed at me. And you. They're everything that's wrong with this town. This *world*."

"And the rabbi? What about him?"

"Ephraim Shwartz cursed himself," Malman said, "the moment he decided to keep that book. It's not my fault he left it lying around. Too afraid to take matters into his own hands, to take the power and *use* it!"

The golem's arms slithered like a pair of serpents. Quinn stepped back, gripping the hammer with both hands.

"They mock us, Quinn. Not to our faces, not always. We are the other. We always have been." He reached into his shirt, lifting a Star of David on a chain. "Do you know how many people in this town came to Ethan's funeral?"

Quinn shook his head.

"Eight. *Eight* of them. If that doesn't tell you what the people of Stark Falls think of you and me, then I don't know what else to say. The golem isn't just to take the ones who came back. I'll have it take everyone. Everyone who sees us as some... some kind of second-class citizens. Everyone who has hatred in their hearts. Ignorance and malice."

"Henry and I were there," Quinn said.

"And my mom," Hector added.

"My folks, too." Wendy said.

"This isn't *about* you, kids." Malman's voice softened. "Please. Just leave us."

"Not until you give them all back."

"I can't!"

Quinn took a deep breath. "Wendy, give me the chisel."

Malman's eyes widened. "What are you doing?"

"Ending this."

"How DARE YOU!"

The golem moved quicker than Quinn could imagine, its gigantic feet carrying its malformed body as if it were gliding instead of running.

"Hit the deck!"

Hector and Wendy dove to either side as the golem's claws lashed out. Quinn ducked, feeling the rush of air as the giant claw sailed over his head. A loud *crack* resounded, and he turned to see the stalactite he'd hidden behind cut in half as if it were made of dough.

"Distract it!" Hector cried. "Hey! Over here! Clay boy!"

"Yeah, yeah you!" Wendy shouted.

"Stay away from him!" Malman screamed.

The golem spun to face them. Quinn saw his chance. With the thing's back turned, he could sneak up, place the chisel, and—

Pain burst through every nerve.

Quinn couldn't take a breath. He fell back hard, tailbone smashing into the ground.

Mr. Malman stood over him.

"Don't make me do this, Quinn. I've never hurt anyone. Don't make me hurt you."

Quinn sucked in a desperate lungful of air. His stomach was cramped so bad he was afraid he'd throw up. He looked up at Mr. Malman and saw a stranger. Broken. Too far gone.

"Mr...Mr. Malman," he wheezed. "Look," he pointed to the golem attacking Wendy and Hector.

"Would Ethan do that?" he asked. "Would Ethan Malman hurt *kids*?"

Malman's face twisted in fury. "That's not—"

"Not what?" Quinn asked, picking himself up. "Not Ethan?"

"You don't know what you're dealing with, Quinn."

"No," Quinn said. "I don't. I didn't read the *Book of Gotzner*. I barely read the Torah. But I don't need to know. All I need to do is *see*. And that...isn't your SON! You think you're the only one who suffered? Henry has nightmares about it. Every night. He cries about Ethan, about how he tried to help him. None of those guys came back...not really. They survived, but they didn't come home *whole*. And everyone else...Maria and Terry and Hank. They can still learn from their mistakes! They can grow. People can *change*. Change for the better. This town *can* be better! But that?" He pointed the hammer towards the golem. "That will only make things worse. Much worse. So I'm going to end it."

He picked up the hammer and chisel and made a run for it, shoving past Malman as the golem grabbed Hector by the front of his poncho, lifting him up like a toy and shaking him. Malman tried to grab for Quinn and missed, tripping on the slick cave floor.

As Hector flailed in the golem's grip, Wendy swung her lantern, bashing it against its other arm. The creature let out a bone shaking howl and threw her across the floor. Wendy uttered a pained cry as she smacked into the cave wall. She charged again, this time with a chisel. Instead of tackling it, she slid like a baseball player sliding into home base. But the golem was too fast and leapt away just in time. Wendy spat out a curse, gathering herself to try again.

"Hey!" Quinn yelled.

The golem turned, its wide mouth dripping puddles at its feet.

Quinn set the chisel against the creature's chest and readied the hammer.

Please, he prayed. *Please, let this be the end of it.*

A powerful hand stayed his arm before he could swing.

Quinn turned and found Mr. Malman behind him, his face grave. His skin looked sick and grey, his blue eyes wet with tears.

"Let it go, Quinn," he said softly.

"Don't listen to him!" Wendy said. "Bash it!"

"Yeah!" Hector replied, still struggling in the golem's grasp.

"I can't," Quinn told him. "He has to be destroyed. It's going to *kill* them."

Malman's fists unclenched, his shoulders slacking. A heavy silence passed for a dozen heartbeats.

"I know," Malman said.

Quinn paused. "You know…what?"

"Give me the hammer, son. And that chisel."

"It's a trick!" Wendy said. "Quinn, don't let go!"

"It's over," Malman said. "Let me be the one to end it." All the fight had left him, and he gave Quinn a pleading look. "Please."

"How can I trust you?" Quinn asked. "After everything you've done. How can I *ever* trust you?"

Malman shook his head, his grip still strong on Quinn's arm. "You can't. I don't suppose you ever will again. But you're right. My Ethan… he wouldn't have done those things. He never hurt people. He saved them. Died saving them. A part of him is inside there, somewhere. But it's hidden too deep. Stuffed down too far." Tears slid through the stubble on his cheeks. "*The Book of Gotzner* warns that after time, golems are harder to control. I didn't think this was true, until I heard about Mr. Gibbs and his daughter. Ethan has...misstepped, sometimes. Done things I never told him to do. Dangerous, reckless things. I was a fool. I *am* a fool. Give me the hammer, Quinn. Let me do my duty as a father."

"Quinn, no!"

Quinn released his grip, letting Mr. Malman take it. He urged Quinn to step aside, then took up the chisel.

"Ethan," he said, his voice hard. "Ethan, I want you to put him down. Now."

Obediently, the golem set Hector down.

"Step aside, Hector."

He walked up to the golem, who crouched down, chittering away, almost happily. Like it craved Malman's approval.

"You've been good," Malman told it. "You've done everything I've asked of you."

The golem cocked its head from one side to the other, its eyes searching Malman's face.

"I need you to do one last thing for me, Ethan. Hold still. Can you do that?"

The golem nodded. As Malman came closer with the hammer and chisel, it closed its eyes.

Quinn watched as Malman positioned the chisel over its chest. Watched the old man shudder as the sobs overtook him.

"It will be okay," he said. "You won't feel a thing."

Softly, Malman began to sing.

"Oh glow-worm, tell me pray, how do you kindle,
   Lamps that by the break of day,
   That by the break of day, must fade and dwindle"

The golem swayed to the sound of Malman's voice.

"There, there," Malman said.

He cried out as he swung the hammer. The chisel exploded into the golem's chest. It let out the loudest, most painful sound Quinn had ever heard. Its face contorted, and just for a moment, he could have sworn he saw an image of Ethan Malman flash across the creature's face.

Malman fell to his knees as the golem began to crumble. Its body fell in chunks, long arms breaking like sticks of chalk, legs snapping like toothpicks. Finally, the head and body collapsed, falling like lumps of ash in a fireplace until nothing was left but a pile of dried clay at Malman's feet.

The cave was silent, save for the sound of rushing water.

The Crypt Crew sat motionless, gazing upon the remains of the golem. Malman reached out a hand and felt the pile, shuddering.

"It's over, now," Wendy said.

The old man didn't look up as Quinn laid a hand on his shoulder.

"I'm sorry," Mr. Malman whispered, and for a moment Quinn didn't know who he was talking to, until he lifted his head to look Quinn in the eyes.

"Quinn, I'm so sorry."

Quinn looked down at the golem's remains. He didn't see a monster. Only the twisted form that Mr. Malman's grief had taken. All of the fears and sadness of a man who thought he was alone in the world, without a friend, without a family, without hope.

He knelt down and hugged him. Mr. Malman hugged him back.

"I'm so, so sorry, son."

They held each other in the cave for a long time, until a faint voice echoed from the tunnel.

"Kids?"

Rabbi Shwartz limped out of the tunnel, using a piece of wood as a makeshift crutch. He paused at the sight of the golem.

"It's over, rabbi," Quinn said.

Rabbi Shwartz came closer. "Yes. *The Book of Gotzner*. Jonas, where—"

"Burned," Mr. Malman said. He nodded to the pile of rubble. "Burned after I made…him."

"For the best," Rabbi Shwartz said. "The others are waking, free of the curse. They'll be here soon."

"And the Deputy?" Malman asked.

The rabbi held out his hands. "I don't know what to tell you, Jonas, other than you have many crimes to answer for."

"Yes, Rebbe," Malman said. "Yes, I do."

The group stood around the golem for a long while, until the sound of several footsteps echoed through the tunnel. Malman patted Quinn on the cheek.

"Thank you," he said.

Quinn reached down, feeling the lumps of clay. He studied one on the palm of his hand, watching as it gently crumbled to dust.

SHINE LITTLE GLOW-WORM, GLIMMER

Ten Months Later
May 1986

The Katz house was packed. Quinn could barely keep up with the congratulations, handshakes, punches to the arm, and the occasional pulling of the yarmulke he'd pinned to the top of his head. His bar mitzvah had gone well, and he'd only faltered twice while standing at the *bimah* and delivering a *d'var Torah*. He was nervous, sure, but seeing Hector, Wendy, and Henry in the crowd calmed his anxiety. All the while, the rabbi looked on approvingly, standing beside him on a brand-new prosthetic leg.

Most of the town had turned up, barely able to squeeze into the small synagogue. Even Mrs. Ruane was there, and only interrupted once when she felt Quinn wasn't speaking loud enough, her ear trumpet at the ready. Terry and Frank snickered behind her, but were quickly shushed by Maria.

"So," Hector was saying as the Crypt Crew stepped out onto the front porch, "you're saying I get to keep this?" He fiddled with his own yarmulke, which kept sliding off his moussed-up hair.

"Of course," Quinn said. "It has my initials and the date, see?" He removed his own and showed Hector the embroidered Q.K. 5/15/86.

"Neat," he said, and went about trying to make his stay on straight.

"Well," a gruff voice said behind them, "feel like a man yet?"

Sheriff Toohey, or ex-Sheriff Toohey, stood in the doorway, his sunburned and freckled face beaming.

"Not quite yet," Quinn said.

"Eh, you never do," Toohey said, taking a long sip of his Arnold Palmer. "We're all just kids, inside." He leaned forward, lowering his voice. "That's the big secret, you know. Ain't no such thing as grownups. Just grown kids." He laughed, gesturing to the Stark Falls Sheriff car parked in the driveway. "Makes me happy, knowing Henry took the job."

"You liked Florida that much, huh?" Wendy asked.

Toohey shrugged. "No snow. Good fishing. Clear water. No mysterious cases of clay men runnin' around causin' a ruckus. Yeah, kids. I like Florida just fine."

Toohey had come back to town a week after the Old Rickety was repaired. Henry had Malman arrested, and called a secret, or not so secret, town meeting, in which he, Mr. Fancis, Dr. Delgado, and Mr. Arpin had put their heads together, deciding what to charge him with. No one had been hurt, save for some cuts and bruises. Property had been damaged, sure.

But people had been kidnapped. Crimes were committed, but there would be no mention of golems, or rabbis with magical books.

In the end, Henry arrested Mr. Malman for breaking and entering, conspiring to kidnap, and disturbing the peace. As soon as the trial took place, he pleaded with the judge for a light sentencing. Malman was sent to a minimum-security prison with a three year sentence. In his absence, Mr. Arpin and Brent Foster took temporary control of Malman & Son's, and business had never been better. They kept the horror magazines stocked, the arcade machines running, and made sure to have the basement sealed.

"Well, it was nice to have you back," Quinn said.

"Had to make the drive," Toohey said. "Couldn't pass up the chance to see my favorite Katz celebrate his bar mitzvah. Mazel tov, eh?"

"Hey, Ed!" Mr. Arpin came out, his saxophone slung over his shoulder. Brent Foster was beside him, clean shaven and smiling. "We're gonna start playing out back. Think you can still work that harmonica of yours?"

"Sure can!" The old Sheriff gave the Crew a wink and slipped back inside.

They stepped off the porch and onto the yard, passing by the Sheriff's car.

"Henry let up with those John Wayne impressions, yet?" Hector asked.

"No way," Quinn said. "If anything, he's doing them more."

Wendy and Hector shared a laugh as Quinn stared at the mailbox.

"What do you think, guys?"

He kept his eyes trained on the small red flag. He'd seen the mail truck pass by as the rabbi was giving his toast in the dining room and almost ran out then and there. He'd been waiting for this day for months.

"I have a good feeling," Wendy said.

"Me too," Hector agreed. He threw an arm around Quinn's shoulder. "We'll look together, yeah?"

"Yeah. Together."

Quinn flipped the lid of the mailbox down. Inside, a package in brown paper tied with twine sat on top of a thick, manila envelope. A new edition of the *Stark Falls Minuteman* hung from the box, the front page a wide shot of Hampton Harwich grinning and waving from a hospital bed.

Pulse racing, Quinn removed the envelope. His hands trembled when he saw what was written in the center:

"Open it," Wendy said, wringing her hands in anticipation.

Quinn took a deep breath and tore the corner of the envelope, slipping out the glossy paper inside. The Crew gathered around as he unfolded the paper:

From the Editors of Tales of Terror Magazine,

Mr. Katz, Ms. Francis, and Mr. Delgado,

Congratulations! It is our great pleasure to inform you that your latest submission has been accepted for publication in our next issue of

TALES OF TERROR. Please accept our heartfelt congratulations. Included is a check in the amount dictated by our author contract. Complimentary copies will be sent to this address as soon as they're off the printers.

We look forward to future submissions from your writing and illustrating team and are very pleased to include your truly terrifying tale, **"CREATURES OF CLAY"**, *in next month's issue. We think it will be quite the scare!*

Best wishes,

TALES OF TERROR

"You guys," Hector said, breathless.

"I know," Wendy said. She was practically vibrating.

"We did it," Quinn said. He held up the letter. "We DID IT!"

"No one stops the Crypt Crew!" Hector cried.

"No one," Wendy agreed.

"Hey!"

Henry was on the porch. "We're having a party for Mr. Quinn Katz here, just in case you were wondering. Wanna bring it inside?"

Behind him, Maria waved from an open window, beaming in her Nature Scout sash covered in new badges. Hector waved back.

"Coming!" Quinn replied.

"Yeah, Sheriff, we're coming!" Hector echoed.

Henry smiled, giving them a salute.

Quinn handed Wendy the letter. He went to shut the mailbox, stopping when he remembered the package. He slid it out.

Quinn's name and address were posted on it in thick lettering, next to **New Hampshire State Prison For Men**. There was no other address. Curious, he undid the twine wrapping. Inside was something in wax paper, round and thin.

A handwritten note slipped out. He caught it with his sneaker before it blew away in the wind.

Quinn,

Mazeltov on your bar mitzvah. I hope you had a wonderful day! Know that you, Hector, and Wendy are never far from my thoughts. I hope you're all doing well. Are you still writing your horror stories? I hope you are. I liked the last ones, you know. Don't think I ever got a chance to tell you. I'm proud of you, son. So very proud. Hope to see you soon. Shalom.

J.M.

He opened the other object wrapped in wax paper. It was a small record, a 45. There was no record sleeve. He flipped the disc over, reading the label:

THE MIDNIGHT CROONERS
   "GLOW-WORM"

Quinn felt a chill, but couldn't tell if it was the record or the early spring breeze. Goosebumps pricked his arms.

He slid the book into his back pocket along with Malman's note. *Best not to ruin the party*, he thought. *I'll tell Henry in the morning.*

A sound in the front yard made him turn back. A familiar sound, one he'd never thought he'd hear again. Chittering, like those fake wind-up dentures in the gag shops. The sound he heard in those dark, muddy tunnels. He looked around, gazing across the empty yard.

"Burned," he whispered.

Wendy and Hector turned to him.

"He said he burned the *Book of Gotzner*, right?"

"Yeah," Hector said. "What's the matter? You look like you've just met the Grim Reaper."

"It's...nothing," Quinn said. "Let's get back to the party. I'm sure the rabbi has some more good stories for us."

As he shut the door, the melody, that haunting melody that seemed to follow him everywhere, began playing in his head. A lilt of four voices crooning.

Shine little glow-worm, glimmer...

Author's Note

On the Golem: If you're reading this book then, like me, you're a fan of monsters. When I thought up Stark Falls, I was at a loss as to which kind should be lurking in the shadows, waiting to terrorize the small town. I knew that the Crypt Crew needed to take on something special for their first foray into the world of terror. Something that would have a personal connection to our hero, Quinn Katz.

For inspiration, I turned to my own cultural folklore and chose a creature that has been fascinating (and often terrifying) people for centuries: the golem.

The clay man, whose Hebrew name means "unfinished" or "incomplete", has been depicted as many things over the years: A protector. A servant. The first true man. And yes, even a monster.

Legend, folklore, obscure texts and secondhand translations have led to a slew of theories as to how the creature came to be.

One particular text, the *Book Yetzirah* or *Book of Creation*, is often cited as a source for the "magical wisdom" of creating life. Written sometime between the 3rd and 6th century CE, the book describes the meaning behind the "thirty two ways of wisdom", which is a combination of the ten *sefiroth* (original numbers) and the 22 consonants of the Hebrew alphabet. Later, it became somewhat of a manual on golem making for Jewish mystics.

This account is written by the students of Rabbi Judah the Pious of Speyer (d. 1217), concerning Jeremiah and his son, Ben Sira:

Ben Sira wished to study the *Book Yetzirah*. Then a heavenly voice went forth: You cannot make him (such a creature) alone. He went to his father Jeremiah. They busied themselves with it, and at the end of three years a man was created to them, on whose forehead stood *emeth*, as on Adam's forehead. Then the man they had made said to them: God alone created Adam, and when he wished to let Adam die, he erased the *aleph* from *emeth* and he remained *meth*, dead. That is what you should do to me: Reverse the combination of letters and erase the aleph of the word *emeth* from my forehead – and he immediately fell into dust."

The notion of the golem morphing into a thing to be feared sprang from Ashkenazi communities in the 15th and 16th centuries, mainly in Poland and Germany. No matter who does the telling, it's clear that the golem has always been a friend and foe combined, able to turn upon its maker in the blink of an eye.

Like Mary Shelley's *Frankenstein*, this next story shows the golem as a dangerous creature, very hard to control. Rabbi Elijah Baal Shem, an expert on "practical Kabbalah", or magic, was the rabbi of Chelm. He died in 1583, but his descendants passed down this story, which was eventually written in 1674 by Christoph Arnold:

"After saying certain prayers and holding certain fast days, they make the figure of a man from clay, and when they have said the *shem hamephorash* over it, the man comes to life. Although the man itself cannot speak, it understands what is said to it and commanded; among the Polish Jews it does all kinds of housework, but it is not allowed to leave the house. On the forehead they write *emeth*, that is, truth. But it grows each day; very small at first, it ends up becoming larger than all those in the house. In order to take away its strength, which ultimately becomes a threat to all those in the house, they quickly erase the *aleph* from its forehead, so there remains only the word *meth*, that is, dead. When this is done, the golem collapses and dissolves into the clay and mud that he was…They say that a *baal shem* in Poland, by the name of Rabbi Elias, made a golem who became so large that the rabbi could no longer reach his forehead to erase the letter *e*. He thought up a trick, namely that the golem, being his servant, should remove his boots, supposing that when the golem bent over, he would erase the letters. And so it happened, but when the golem became mud again, his whole weight fell on the rabbi, who was sitting on the bench, and crushed him."

Ouch.

The most famous golem is, of course, the Golem of Prague.

Legend has it that the Rabbi Judah Loew ben Bezalel, the 16th century rabbi of Prague, created a golem to defend the Jewish ghetto from anti-Semitic attacks and pogroms. Rabbi Loew kept the golem in control by removing the *shem* before the Sabbath. The most popular version of the story has Rabbi Loew forgetting to remove the *shem*, which causes the golem to fly into a rampage. Eventually, the rabbi finally manages to remove it, causing the golem to fall to pieces.

Some say the remains of the golem are still stored in the attic of the Old New Synagogue, where it waits to be reactivated if the Jews ever need another defender.

While researching various stories of the golem, I noticed something curious: Not *once* does someone create a golem with the express purpose of causing evil. If golems are mindless automaton bound to their maker's bidding, what would it look like if their makers were spiteful, misguided, filled with hate?

In fiction, no villain should be evil for evil's sake. Yet I still wanted to play with the idea of making a golem to cause harm. Rabbi Gotzner makes his to seek revenge, much like Mr. Malman does decades later. There is, however, a slight difference, as Malman also uses the golem as a replacement for his deceased son.

This is inspired by a Yiddish and Slavic folktale similar to *The Gingerbread Man*, called *The Clay Boy*, in which an elderly couple bake a boy out of clay to as a stand in for a real child. Like most golem stories, it ends with the Clay Boy growing less and less hard to control, eventually going on a rampage, eventually growing to a monstrous size and eating the couple.

The golem has turned up in film a few times, most notably in *The Golem: How He Came Into the World* (1920), widely considered to be a classic in the horror genre, and the inspiration for the screen version of Universal's *Frankenstein*. Another fun one which I highly recommend is the British cult classic *It!* (1967), in which a museum curator uses a newly found golem to destroy his enemies, using a shem much like rabbi Loew from the Prague legend.

While I've taken bits and pieces of the legend various eras, the golems in this story are purely fictional, more akin to zombies, vampires, or Frankenstein's Monster than the beings found in Jewish folklore. I have kept the idea of writing *meth* on the golem, but in this book, it is written on the chest, not the forehead. Instead of erasing the letter from the golem itself, Rabbi Shwartz and the Crypt Crew use weapons inscribed with the word *meth*, or death, and strike it in the chest (much like a stake through the heart of a vampire). The concept is still the same, but the method is much more dramatic.

The rules and rites concerning their creation also differ. I make no mention of any texts like the *Zohar* of the *Book Yetsirah*, instead choosing to create a fictitious book that claims to contain all the pooled knowledge of golem making, the *Book of Gotzner*.

Like the *Necronomicon* of Lovecraftian and *Evil Dead* lore, *The Book of Gotzner* serves as a manual for summoning all sorts of evil, be it demons from ancient Babylon to the feared sheddims: monsters and demons of Assyrian and Semetic history.

The way the golems can "turn" others is another of my creations. While soulless, the idea of them being forced to turn humans into yet more golems without the aid of a rabbi was a terrifying and interesting concept to me. Something akin to vampires running amok, or a group of gorgons on the prowl.

Though they're only as dangerous as their creators intend them to be, I set out to build upon the idea of the golem as a monster, misunderstood and deadly, and strove to make them as scary as possible.

I hope I succeeded.

On the setting: I chose to set the book in a small New England town for several reasons.

Stark Falls, with its small but varied population, is my own social petri dish. A place that I could play with social norms, the idea of being an "outsider" in a very buttoned up society, and the problem of deep-rooted, small-town ignorance.

It might shock us today that Jews were still looked at as "the other", especially in a place like America, home to so much of the world's

Jewish population, with the Holocaust a mere 40 years in the past. I wish I could say that attitudes have changed, but anti-Semitism doesn't seem to be going away any time soon. I hope this story, in whatever small way it can, helps in the fight to change that.

I wrote Quinn as a Jewish boy who initially rejects his faith, but has to finally embrace his roots, something that I went through a bit later in life. Now, more than ever, I think kids need to see Jewish heroes in action.

Acknowledgments

My sincere thanks to Alison Weiss, who believed in Quinn and the rest of the Crypt Crew from the very start and helped whip their story into shape.

Zach Friday, for his keen editorial eye, creative input, and just a real pleasure to work with.

Geo Kennedy for his amazing artwork. You really brought the Crypt Crew to life, and I'll be forever grateful.

I'd also like to thank some friends who (unbeknownst to some), let me borrow their names, including Matt Arpin, John Francis, Eric Castelot, Dave Ward, and Ken Willette. There are more of you in there, but you'll have to read for yourselves. I figured it would be a nice surprise.

For my father, Patrick Moody Sr., who never gave up on me and continues to be a bastion of encouragement and inspiration.

My sister, Emma Moody, who would have been a shoe in in the Crypt Crew on her own accord.

Maggie Jenson, the greatest aunt, a true artist, and my biggest champion.

My wife, Megan, who inspires me every day.

Last but not least, I would like to acknowledge the work of the writers and artists of *EC Comics*, revolutionaries who were truly ahead of their time, as well as Forry Ackerman, editor of *Famous Monsters of Filmland*, and every late night horror host who graced the screen on those dark and stormy nights in the long ago days of my youth. Without them, there would be no Quinn, Hector, or Wendy.

About the Author

Patrick Moody is the author of one previous novel, *The Gravedigger's Son*. His short fiction has appeared in numerous anthologies, including *Halloween Horror Vol. 2*, *A Monster Told Me Bedtime Stories: MONSTERS Volume 7*, *Lovecraft In A Time of Madness*, and *Kentucky Fried Horror*, among others. His work has also been adapted into audio dramas on several podcasts, including *Campfire Radio Theater* and *The Wicked Library*. He and his wife live outside New Haven, Connecticut.

Milton Keynes UK
Ingram Content Group UK Ltd.
UKHW021046020524
442115UK00013B/365